VLAD

VLAD

CARLOS FUENTES

TRANSLATED BY
E. SHASKAN BUMAS AND
ALEJANDRO BRANGER

DALKEY ARCHIVE PRESS
CHAMPAIGN / DUBLIN / LONDON

Originally published in Spanish as *Vlad* by Alfaguara, Mexico City, 2010
An excerpt from this translation originally appeared in *Playboy* Magazine
Copyright © 2004, 2012 by Carlos Fuentes
Translation copyright © 2012 by E. Shaskan Bumas and Alejandro Branger
First edition, 2012

Library of Congress Cataloging-in-Publication Data

Fuentes, Carlos.
 [Vlad. English]
 Vlad / Carlos Fuentes ; translated by E. Shaskan Bumas and Alejandro Branger. -- 1st
ed.
   p. cm.
 ISBN 978-1-56478-779-8 (cloth : acid-free paper)
 1. Vlad III, Prince of Wallachia, 1430 or 31-1476 or 7--Fiction. 2. Vampires--Fiction. 3.
Mexico--Fiction. I. Bumas, E. Shaskan, 1961- II. Branger, Alejandro. III. Title.
 PQ7297.F793V5313 2012
 863'.64--dc23

                          2012006983

Partially funded by a grant from the Illinois Arts Council, a state agency.

La presente traducción fue realizada con el estímulo del Programa de Apoyo a la Traducción de Obras Mexicanas a Lenguas Extranjeras (Protrad), dependiente de las institu-
ciones culturales de México convocantes.

This translation was carried out with the support of the Program to Support the Translation of Mexican Works into Foreign Languages (ProTrad), with the collective support of
Mexico's cultural institutions.

www.dalkeyarchive.com

Cover: design and composition by by Nicholas Motte

To Cecilia, Rodrigo, and Gonzalo,
the child monsterologists of Sarria

Go to sleep, my girl,
here comes the coyote;
coming to get you
with a great garrote

—Mexican lullaby

1

"I wouldn't trouble you, Navarro, if Dávila and Uriarte were available. I'm not going to call them your inferiors—*subordinates* sounds better—but neither will I forget that you are a senior partner, *primus inter pares*, and so are higher ranked in this firm. I am entrusting this task to you because, first and foremost, I consider this a matter of utmost urgency . . ."

Weeks later, when the awful adventure had ended, I recalled that, at its beginning, I had chalked up the absence of Dávila and Uriarte to luck. Dávila was off on his honeymoon in Europe, and Uriarte was tied up in a judicial embargo. As for me, I was neither going away on a wedding trip, nor would I have ordinarily accepted the work, appropriate for a lawyer just out of school, that our boss had delegated to our indefatigable Uriarte.

But I respected the decision of my elderly employer and appreciated the meaningful intimacy of his trust. He had always been an uncompromising man whose decisions were final. He was not in the habit of asking anyone for advice. Although he was tactful enough to listen attentively to his co-workers' points of view, he replied with orders. And yet, in spite of what I just said, how could I ignore the peculiar circumstances by which he'd acquired his fortune? His status as a rich man was recent enough for him still to be considered "new money," but even that new money, thanks to the gravitas of its owner, felt every bit as old as his eighty-nine years and tied to the history of an already buried century. His wealth was largely a result of the obsequiousness (or the moral flexibility) with which he had served (and risen in his service of) successive governmental administrations during his long years in Mexico. Suffice it to say he was an "influential man."

I must confess that I never saw my boss behave submissively to anyone. I could only guess at the inevitable concessions that his haughty gaze and already curved spine had been forced to make—over the course of his career—to politicians who could hardly be said to exist at all beyond the six-year span of a president's term. He knew perfectly well that political power was fleeting; the officials did not. They prided themselves on having been named ministers for six years, after which they would be forgotten for the rest of their lives; whereas the admirable thing about the distinguished Don Eloy Zurinaga, Esq., was that for sixty years he had known how to slither from one presidential administration to the next while always landing on his feet. His strategy was quite simple. Throughout his career, he never fell out with politicians because he never once let them glimpse the inevitability of their political greatness dwindling to a future of insignificance. Few saw past the superficial courtesy and empty praise of Eloy Zurinaga's ironic smile.

As for his attitude toward me, I quickly accepted that if it did not behoove him to display any new loyalties, this was because he never demonstrated any lasting affection to anyone or to anything. That is, his official conduct was professional: honest and efficient. It can only remain a matter of conjecture whether that honesty was genuine and that efficiency just a type of tyranny, and whether both qualities combined into a mask necessary for survival in the swamp of political and judicial corruption. If

Licenciado Zurinaga never quarreled with a government official, that was probably because he'd never much liked any of them. He didn't need to say this. His life, his career, even his dignity confirmed it.

A year had passed since Mr. Zurinaga, my boss, had become housebound. In all that time, nobody at the firm ever dared imagine that the physical absence of the man in charge allowed for slack behavior, tardiness, or idle jokes. On the contrary, in his absence, Zurinaga felt all the more present. He seemed to have issued a warning: "Be careful. At any moment I might show up and surprise you. Watch out."

More than once during the past year, Mr. Zurinaga had telephoned to announce his imminent arrival in the office. Although he never showed up, on each occasion a holy terror put the entire staff on high alert, leaving us all on our best behavior. And then, one morning, an individual who seemed identical to the boss came into, and a half hour later left, the office. The only reason we knew it wasn't really him was that in the course of that half hour, Mr. Zurinaga telephoned a few times to issue instructions. On the phone that morning, he spoke in a decisive, almost dictatorial way, without entertaining a single question, remark, or response. Then, without allowing for so much as an acknowledgment, he hung up. Word spread that the individual in the office couldn't be the boss after all, and yet, when he walked out, seen from behind, he was tall and stooped over, just like the absent lawyer. He was dressed in an old polo coat with its lapels lifted to his ears and a totally out-of-fashion black-and-brown felt hat from which two uncontrolled white tufts of hair burst like the wings of a bird.

The walk, the cough, and the clothing were all the boss's, but this visitor, who entered the *sancta sanctorum* of the office with such nonchalance that nobody stopped him, was not Eloy Zurinaga. The joke—if it even was a joke—didn't leave any of us laughing. Quite the opposite. The appearance of this double, specter, or look-alike— whatever he was—only made us feel unease and anxiety.

Because he no longer came into the office, my meetings with the lawyer Eloy Zurinaga, my boss, took place at his home. From the street, a skimpy and miserable garden led to an equally miserable, collapsing set of stairs to the great house. He lived in one of the last remaining Porfirian mansions, as they're called, in reference to the dictatorship of General Porfirio Díaz, specifically the period from 1884 to 1910, our pretend belle époque. For some unknown reason, no one had torn down the mansion, unlike the rest of the Roma neighborhood of Mexico City, which has been razed to make way for office buildings, condominiums, and shops. One needed only enter the large, ramshackle two-storied house, crowned with a mansard roof and atop an inaccessible cellar, to understand that the lawyer's entrenchment was not a matter of will so much as one of gravity. Zurinaga had accumulated so many papers, books, case files, pieces of furniture, bibelots, dishes, paintings, rugs, tapestries, folding screens, and especially memories in that residence that to change locations would have been for him like changing his life and accepting, even hastening, his death.

To demolish the house would be to demolish his entire existence.

Zurinaga's obscure origins (or his cold reasoning, devoid of sentimental concessions) excluded from the gray stone mansion any reference to family. The interior lacked any pictures of women, parents, children, or friends. Instead, the house was crammed with an overabundance of old-fashioned decorative objects that gave the place the feeling of an antiques warehouse: Sèvres vases, Dresden figurines, bronze nudes and marble busts, flimsy chairs with gilded backrests, Biedermeier-style tables, heavy armchairs of burnished leather, along with the intrusion here and there of art-nouveau lamps . . . This was a house without the slightest hint of feminine grace.

Instead, hanging on the red velvet-lined walls were artistic treasures that, seen up-close and taken together, revealed a shared macabre quality: disturbing engravings by the Mexican Julio Ruelas of heads drilled by monstrous insects; phantasmagoric paintings by the Swiss Henry Füssli, whose specialty was the depiction of nightmares, of distortions, the marriage of sex and horror, females and fear . . .

"Just imagine," the attorney Zurinaga smiled. "Füssli was a cleric who fell out with an ecclesiastical judge. The judge defrocked him, and that's what pushed Füssli toward art . . ."

Zurinaga brought his fingers together beneath his chin.

"Sometimes, I would like to have been a judge who expelled himself from the judiciary and so is condemned to art . . . Too late," he sighed. "For me, life has become a long parade of corpses . . . My only comfort is to count those who have not yet left, those who age with me . . ."

Sunken in his leather wing chair worn from years of use, Zurinaga caressed its arms the way another man might caress the arms of a woman. His long white fingers took such deliberate pleasure from this that the lawyer seemed to be saying: "The flesh decays; the chair endures. Take your pick: one skin or the other."

Zurinaga was seated near a fireplace that was lit day and night, even in warm weather, as if cold were a state of mind, something like the spiritual temperature of the boss's soul.

His pale face revealed a network of blue veins, giving him a translucent though healthy appearance in spite of the minute web of wrinkles that spread between his balding cranium and his well-shaved chin, forming tiny eddies of old flesh around his lips and thick curtains above his gaze that, in spite of everything, was penetrating and watchful—even more so, perhaps, because his aged flesh had caused his pitch-black eyes to sink deep into his skull.

"So, how do you like my house, counselor?"

"Very much, Don Eloy."

"A dreary mansion, large beyond all need . . ." the old lawyer recited in a strange trance. He was a rare bird, considering his species—I thought as I listened to him—a Mexican lawyer who quoted English poetry. The old man smiled again.

"So you see, my dear Yves Navarro, the advantage of living a long life is the opportunity to learn more than one's circumstances alone would allow."

"Circumstances?" I asked in good faith, not certain what Zurinaga was talking about.

"Sure," he said as he brought together his long pale fingers. "You descend from a great family; I ascend from an unknown tribe. You have forgotten what your ancestors knew. I have learned what mine never knew."

He extended his hand and again caressed the beautiful worn leather of his comfortable armchair. I laughed: "Don't be so sure. Being a wealthy landowner in the nineteenth century in no way guaranteed a cultivated mind. More likely the opposite! My forefathers had a hacienda in Querétaro where they grew maguey and fermented it to make *pulque* liquor. That sort of operation wouldn't have been especially conducive to the enlightenment of its owners, that's for sure."

The light from the burning logs played on our faces like murky remains of sunlight.

"My ancestors were not interested in knowing," I added, "just in owning."

"Have you ever asked yourself, Licenciado Navarro, why the so-called 'upper classes' in Mexico never hang on to their stations long?"

"It must be a sign of the country's health, Don Eloy. It means that there's social mobility in Mexico, movement, the possibility of bettering one's position: a permeability of class boundaries. Those of us who lost everything during the Revolution—and we had a lot to lose—not only accepted it, we applauded the fact."

Eloy Zurinaga rested his chin on his clasped hands and looked at me with understanding.

"The problem is that, in the Americas, we are all colonials. Here only the Indians can be true aristocrats. The European conquistadors, the colonizers, were commoners, the hoi polloi, ex-cons . . . On the other side of the ocean, the Old World bloodlines prolong themselves, not only because they date back centuries, but also because they don't depend, like we do, on immigration. Take Germany. No Hohenstaufen had to cross the Atlantic to make his fortune. Think of the Balkans, of Central Europe . . . The Hungarian Arpads date back to 886, for Saint Stephen's sake! The great Župan Vladimir brought the Serbian tribes together in the ninth century, and beginning in 1196 the Numantian Dynasty ruled from the Zeta plain to the region of Macedonia. None of them needed to come to America to make a new start . . ."

Every conversation with Don Eloy Zurinaga was interesting. Yet I knew from experience that the lawyer never spoke without a specific ulterior motive, stealthily approached through far-flung references. I've already mentioned that he was never curt with anyone, neither with his inferiors nor with his superiors; however, being so very superior himself, Zurinaga didn't admit that there could be anyone above him. In any case, it was true: he paid polite attention to those of us who were beneath him, allowing us all to say our piece.

But when, following this pleasant introduction, my boss got to the point, I wasn't at all surprised at the direction our conversation took.

"Navarro," he said, "I want you to take care of a very important matter."

I nodded in assent.

"We were talking about Central Europe, about the Balkans."

I nodded again.

"An old friend of mine, displaced by wars and revolutions, has lost his estate along the Hungarian-Romanian border. He had extensive lands strewn with castles in ruins. The thing is," said Zurinaga with a touch of melancholy, "the war only exterminated what was already dead."

I looked at him in hope of an explanation.

"As you know, it's preferable to be the master of your own downfall rather than to find yourself the victim of forces beyond your control . . . Suffice it to say that my good friend was the master of his own fall from nobility, and that now, between the fascists and the communists, he's been stripped of his lands and his castles and his . . ."

For the first time in our relationship, I felt that Don Eloy was hesitating. I even noticed a nervous twitch in his left temple.

"Forgive me, Navarro. These are the recollections of an old man. My friend and I are of the same generation. Imagine, we studied together at the Sorbonne back when law, like good manners, was learned in French. Before *l'anglais* corrupted everything," he concluded with bitterness.

He looked at the flames in the fireplace as if to temper his own gaze, and continued with his usual voice, a voice that sounded like a river churning up rocks.

"It just so happens that my old friend has decided to settle in Mexico. You see how easily generalizations fade. My friend's ancestral estate has been his, his family's, since medieval times, and yet, here you have him in Mexico City, seeking a roof over his head."

"How may I be of service, Don Eloy?" I asked hastily.

The old man stared at his trembling hands as he moved them closer to the fire. Then he laughed.

"Would you believe it? Usually, the person who takes care of such matters as these would be Dávila, who, as we know, is away fulfilling more pleasant duties at the moment. And as for Uriarte, between you and me, *ne s'y connaît pas trop* . . . Anyway, the fact is that I am going to entrust you with finding a house for my immigrant friend . . ."

"Only too happy to help, sir, but I . . ."

"No, no. I am not just asking you for a simple favor. I've taken into account that you have a French mother, that you speak the language, and that you are familiar with the culture of the Hexagon. I could not have hoped for a more perfect match for my friend."

He paused and gave me a friendly look.

"Can you imagine? We were students together at the Sorbonne. That means we're of the same generation. He

21

comes from an old Central European family. They owned a great deal of land in the Balkans, between the Danube and the Bistrica neighborhood of Novi Sad, before the devastation of the great wars . . ."

For the first time, staring off as though he was in a sort of trance, Zurinaga had repeated himself. He had only just told me more or less the same thing. I didn't call attention to this excusable symptom of old age.

"Sir," I was quick to say, "I have always followed your instructions."

He stroked my hand. His hand was, in spite of the fire, ice.

"Please, don't think of this as an order," he smiled. "It's more like a happy coincidence. How is Asunción?"

Once again, Zurinaga had disconcerted me. I hadn't expected him to mention my wife.

"Fine, sir, fine."

"What a happy coincidence," the old man repeated. "You are a lawyer in my firm. She has a real estate agency. *Huzzah!* as they used to say. *Huzzah!* Between the two of you, my friend's housing problem is already solved."

2

Asunción and I always breakfast together. First she takes our ten-year-old daughter, Magdalena, to school, and by the time I've showered, shaved, and dressed, she's come back. Because we will be separated until dinnertime, we look forward to breakfast together, and we make it last. Candelaria, our maid and cook, has been with us forever, and before that she was with my wife's family. Asunción's father was an honest notary public. Her mother was a woman with no imagination. Candelaria on the other hand has imagination to burn. Nowhere in the world are breakfasts as satisfying as they are in Mexico, and Candelaria confirms this tenet every morning with a tableful of mangoes, sapodillas, papayas, and mamey sapotes, which prepare the palate for a heavenly feast of chilaquiles in green sauce, huevos rancheros, tamales costeños wrapped in banana leaves, and piping-hot coffee, accompanied by a variety of pastries suggestively described as conches, frogs, powdery shortbread, and hammocks.

A breakfast that lasts an hour, as it should, is a luxury nowadays. For me, it lays the foundation for the day. Breakfast is a time of loving stares that contain the unspoken memory of nocturnal love, and which goes beyond— but includes—culinary pleasure, recalling Asunción in the nude, surrendering to me, and glowing in response to the intensity of my love. Asunción with her perfect and beautiful form, supple to the touch, passionate gaze, yes, ice caught fire . . .

Asunción is my reverse image. Her hair is long, straight, and dark. My hair is short, curly, and chestnut-brown. Her skin is white and soft; her body, curvaceous. My skin color is cinnamon, and I am trim. Her eyes are pitch black. Mine are blue-green. In her thirties, Asunción preserves the dark and youthful luster of her hair. In my forties, I have premature grays. Our daughter, Magdalena, resembles me more than she does her mother. This is all but a law of inheritance: sons favor their mothers; daughters favor their fathers. The girl's untamable hair used to irritate my mother-in-law. Magdalena's nappy hair—her grandmother proclaimed, staring at me with her habitual suspicion—would betray her dark race. The good woman wanted to iron her granddaughter's hair. She died of apoplexy, although her illness was mistaken for a deep comatose state, and the doctors hesitated before pronouncing her dead. Her husband, my father-in-law, reacted to the doctors' assessment of his wife as comatose with ill-concealed alarm, then let out a great sigh of relief when he knew for sure that she was indeed gone. He didn't last long without her, though. As if taking revenge from the other world, Doña Rosalba de la Llave condemned her husband, the notary Don Ricardo, to live, from that day on, in a state of confusion, not knowing where to find his pajamas or his toothpaste, nor knowing what time it was, or even worse, where he'd left his wallet and his briefcase. He was bewildered to death.

Our daughter, Magdalena, has grown up, therefore, having retained her naturally curly hair; her almond-shaped emerald-green eyes strangely flecked with silver; her skin, a mixture of her mother's and father's complexions, the pale of the moon; and at the age of ten, a lovely figure, still childlike, neither chubby nor skinny, filled-out, huggable, scrumptious . . . Her mother doesn't allow her to wear pants; she insists on plaid skirts, and blue cardigans over white blouses—like the well-educated girls from the French School, the *jeune filles*, or "fine mares," of the Mexican upper classes—ankle socks, and patent leather shoes.

All this gives Magdalena an air not exactly doll-like, but old-fashioned, the air of a girl from another time. I see her little classmates dressed in sweatshirts and jeans, and I ask myself whether Asunción is testing our daughter's adaptability to the modern world. (This tension between the modern and the antique was also a point of contention, this time with *my* mother. Being French, she insisted we name the girl Madeleine, but Asunción prevailed; her grandmother could call her anything she liked, Madeleine or even the atrocious Madó, but at home she would always be Magdalena or, at least, Magda.) The fact is that Asunción is the keeper of the sacred flame of tradition, she accepts modern fashions with difficulty, and she herself dresses the way she would like our daughter to dress when she grows up: black tailored suit, dark stockings, and medium heels.

This is our everyday life. I need to emphasize, however, that this is not our normal life, because there can be no normal life for a couple that has lost a son. Didier, our little twelve-year-old boy, died four years ago in a moment of irreparable destiny. Brave and adventurous ever since he was a small child, Didier had been a strong swimmer. Because of his talent for all mechanical and practical tasks, from bicycling to mountain climbing—he pleaded for his own motorcycle—he thought the very sea would have to respect his nonchalant expertise. One afternoon in Acapulco, at the Pie de la Cuesta beach, he ran, whooping with joy, into the ocean's giant waves and strong, invisible undertow.

We never saw him again. The sea never returned him. And so his absence was doubled. Asunción and I do not have any memory, as terrible as it would be, of a dead body. Didier dissolved into the ocean, and I am incapable of hearing the break of a wave without thinking that a trace of my son, turned to salt and foam, is coming back to us, after circulating incessantly, like a ghost ship, from ocean to ocean . . . We try to fix him in our memory as he appears in the photos of his childhood and especially in the final images of his short life. He looked like a younger version of his mother, turned into a little boy. Pale, with large black eyes and thick straight hair that fell naturally over the back of his neck and was beautifully trimmed to dangle over his broad forehead. But it's hard to find a portrait in which he is smiling. Whenever someone with a camera asked him to smile, he protested, "I refuse to look goofy!" a disconcerting amount of dignity in such a little boy. He took his talent for sports so seriously it might have been life itself. And it was. It was life. His life was gone. Away. From us.

We aren't particularly religious, Asunción and I. My maternal family of French Huguenots never yielded to Catholicism, but I have caught Asunción, more than once, speaking to a photograph of Didier, or murmuring, alone, words of love and longing for our son. I only do so in silence.

We needed to forget the animosity that brought us to each other's throats when Didier disappeared. Asunción had wanted to dredge the sea, to explore the whole coastline, to excavate the beach, and to rip open the rocks. She would have drained the ocean until it revealed the boy's body. I pleaded for serenity and acceptance: "I don't want to see him again," I begged, to Asunción's deep offense, "I want to remember him the way he was . . ."

I'll never forget that awful look she shot at me, its disgust and resentment. We never discussed the matter again.

This absence that is a presence. This silence that seeks voice. This portrait forever trapped in childhood . . .

3

To put things another way, when we sit for breakfast, we're already dressed for work. I offer these details about our formal appearances to contrast them with our nocturnal passions. At night in our marital bed, Asunción is like the salamander of myth; cold that shall burn, burning that shall freeze; fleeting like mercury and stable as a precious pearl; devoted, mysterious, surprising, flirtatious; imagined and imaginative . . . No talk, all action. In the morning, we take our breakfast, and we assume our professional roles, still holding onto the memory of a passionate night and feeling the desire for the next night while experiencing both the happiness of having Magdalena and the hurt of having lost Didier.

When I told Asunción about the lawyer Zurinaga's request, she was as pleased as I that this assignment would bring us together through work.

"Zurinaga's friend is looking for a remote house on a lot with yards on all sides, easy to defend against intruders, and get this, with a ravine out back."

"No problem," said Asunción, smiling. "What's with that look, huh? You don't believe me? There are tons of houses like that in Bosques de las Lomas."

"There's more," I went on. "Our client stipulates that all the windows in the house be blacked out."

Her surprise gave me pleasure.

"No windows?"

"That's right. No windows. We have to block them, brick them up, however you say it."

"He wants to live in the dark?"

"Apparently he can only stand artificial light. He has a problem with his eyes."

"Maybe he's albino."

"Nope, I think it's called photophobia. And there's one more thing. He wants us to dig a tunnel between his house and the ravine."

"A tunnel? Our client is a little eccentric."

"A tunnel that connects his house to the ravine so he can go out without having to step foot on the street."

"Make that *very* eccentric. So do you know him?"

"Know him? No, he isn't in the country yet. He's waiting for the house to be ready before he moves here. You find the house, and I'll write up the contracts. Zurinaga gets the bills for the rehab and the furnishings."

"That's odd. That must mean they're pretty close friends."

"Seems like it. But it wasn't just odd, it was a little creepy: when Don Eloy said good-bye to me . . ."

"Creepy how?"

"He said good-bye, but he didn't so much as look at me."

"He did what? Don Eloy?"

"He was looking down at his lap the whole time."

"Darling, you're making too much of that. It sounds like nothing," she assured me. "So tell me, is our client going to live all alone?"

"No, not all alone. He has a manservant and a daughter."

"How old?"

"I don't know about the manservant," I smiled, "but Don Eloy said the girl's ten years old."

"She's ten. That's great. She could be a playmate for Magdalena."

"We'll have to see about that. Does it strike you as odd that our client is the same age as Don Eloy, almost ninety-years old, and he has a ten-year-old daughter?"

"She could be adopted."

"Or the old guy is popping Viagra," I joked.

"Don't worry so much," said my wife in a professional tone. "I'll talk to Alcayaga, the engineer, about the tunnel. You remember, he's Chepina's dad, you know, Magdalena's little friend?"

Afterward we went our separate ways to work: Asunción to her real estate agency in the Polanco area and I to the ancient office that Zurinaga's practice had always occupied, and would always occupy, on Cinco de Mayo Avenue in the historic downtown of our even more ancient Hispano-Aztec city. Asunción's schedule was flexible enough to allow her the luxury of picking up Magdalena from school at five. I'd be back home by seven. Asunción ate alone at her desk, a coffee and a sandwich, never kept company by any clients with whom she might share some familiarity. I, on the contrary, granted myself the Mexican national luxury of a multi-course two-to-three-hour lunch with my friends at the Danubio on Uruguay Street, if I stayed downtown, or otherwise at one of the establishments in the Zona Rosa, preferably the Bellinghausen. At night, at eight sharp, we would put our little girl to bed, listen to her account of the day, tell her bedtime stories, and only when she was asleep, Asunción of my soul, the night was ours, with all of its doubts and its debts . . .

4

The steps for finding our client a home were duly undertaken. Asunción located an available house matching the client's specifications in the mountainous neighborhood of Lomas Heights. I drew up the contracts and presented them to Don Eloy Zurinaga, who in turn, and contrary to his usual practice, took charge himself of ordering the furniture for the house in a style that was the opposite of his own antiquated taste. Free of Victorian or Neo-Baroque bump-outs, very Roche-Bobois in décor, the Lomas mansion evoked a modern monastery, all right angles and views without clutter. Large empty spaces—floors, walls, ceilings—and comfortable, svelte chairs and couches in black leather. Opaque tables of leaden metal. Not one painting, photo, or even a mirror. The house was built for light, in keeping with the principles of Scandinavian design, designed for environments where great openings were required to let in even a little light, but rather out of place in the sunny reality of Mexico. It's no wonder that a great Mexican architect like Ricardo Legorreta builds protective shade into his houses to allow for a cool interior, light in color. But I digress: my boss's client had exiled natural light from this glass palace; he wanted to wall himself in as though in one of his mythical Central European castles, of which Don Eloy had spoken.

Coincidentally, the day that Zurinaga ordered the windows blocked, a veil of clouds had left the house in shadows, and the sparseness of the furnishings was revealed as a necessary deprivation—the better to allow a person to walk around in the dark without tripping over and bumping into everything. A strange detail caught my attention then, because it seemed to compensate for the otherwise stark decor: a great number of drains ran along the walls of the ground floor, as though our client was expecting a flood any day now.

The tunnel was dug from the back of the house to the steep ravine, in accord with the future resident's instructions, and part of the latter's slope stripped bare, harvested of its ancient willows and Montezuma cypresses.

"In whose name should I make out the contracts, sir?" I asked Don Eloy Zurinaga.

"In my name," he said, "as proxy."

"The power-of-attorney document seems to be missing."

"Then draft it, Navarro."

"Fine, but I'll still need the name of the legal tenant."

The lawyer Eloy Zurinaga—so forthright but so cold, so courteous but so distant—now hesitated again, the second time he had ever done so in my presence. But no sooner had he lowered his head involuntarily than he collected himself, cleared his throat, tightened his grip on his armchair, and said in a calm voice: "Vladimir Radu. Count Vladimir Radu."

"All my friends call me Vlad," said our client, smiling, one night a month later, when, already settled into the house in Lomas, he had summoned me for our first meeting.

"I hope you can excuse my eccentric schedule," he went on, courteously extending a hand, inviting me to sit down on a black leather sofa. "In wartime one is forced to live by night and to pretend that nothing is ever happening in one's own dwelling, Monsieur Navarro: that it is uninhabited; that everyone has fled. One must not attract attention."

He paused reflectively. "I understand that you speak French, Monsieur Navarro."

"Yes, my mother was a Parisian."

"Excellent. We will understand each other all the better."

"But as you say, one must not attract attention . . ."

"You're right. You may call me *señor* if you like."

"Mexicans find the *monsieur* pretentious and annoying."

"I see your point."

What did he see? Count Vlad was dressed more like a bohemian, an actor, or an artist than like an aristocrat. He wore all black: black turtleneck shirt, black pants, and black moccasins without socks. His ankles were extremely thin, as was his whole body, but his head was enormous, extra-large but strangely undefined, as though a hawk had disguised itself as a raven, so beneath his artificially placid features, one could all but make out a deeper face that the count had, impossibly, managed to obscure.

Frankly, he looked like a ridiculous marionette. His mahogany-colored hairpiece slid sideways, so he constantly had to adjust it. His overflowing ranchero-style mustache—drooping, rural, shapeless, obviously glued on his upper lip—managed to conceal our client's mouth, depriving him of those expressions of joy, anger, mockery, and affection that the corners of our mouths frame and, at times, betray. But if the mustache was a disguise, the black sunglasses were the true mask; they completely masked his gaze; they didn't leave the slightest opening for the light; they fit too tightly over where his eyes must have been and wrapped mercilessly around his tiny, childish, and scarred ears, giving the impression that Count Vlad had been the victim of several botched face-lifts.

His hands were eloquent. He moved them with disagreeable elegance, he closed them with sudden strength, and he didn't attempt to conceal the strange abnormality of his long glassy nails, as transparent as his windows before he'd had his house sealed.

"Thank you for agreeing to meet with me," he said in a deep, manly, and melodic voice.

I nodded to indicate that I was happy to be of service.

"Can I get you something to drink?" he added right away.

"Perhaps a little red wine," I accepted out of politeness, "if you'll be joining me."

"I never drink," said the Count, with a theatrical pause, "wine." As he sat on a black leather ottoman, he asked, "Do you ever get nostalgic for your ancestral home?"

"I never knew it. The Zapatistas burned down the haciendas, and now they're all fancy hotels, or *paradores* as the Spaniards called them . . ."

He continued as though he hadn't heard me: "I must tell you that, above all, I do feel a need for my ancestral home. But my land has become impoverished, there have been too many wars, and there are no resources left to survive upon there . . . Zurinaga told me a lot about you, Navarro. Haven't you ever lamented the misfortune of old families, made to endure and to maintain tradition?"

"No," I said, allowing the hint of a smile to help shape my words, "not really."

"There are some types of families that become lethargic," he went on, again as though he hadn't heard me, "and they settle all too easily for what they refer to as modern life. Life, Navarro! Does this brief passage, this instant between the womb and the tomb, even deserve to be called life?"

"You're making me nostalgic," I said, in an effort to be amusing, "for the good old days of feudalism."

He tilted his head to one side and adjusted his toupee. "Where does our inexplicable sadness come from? It must have a reason, a cause, a source. Do you know? We're an exhausted people: so much internecine warfare, so much blood spilled for nothing . . . Such sorrow! Everything contains the seed of its own ruin. In things, that ruin is called decay. In people it's called death."

My client's digressions made his conversation difficult to follow. There was little opportunity for small talk with the Count, and metaphysical statements about life and death have never been my specialty. As though to illustrate his morbid point, quick-witted Vlad (as in "Call me Vlad" and "All my friends call me Vlad") walked over to the piano where he played Chopin's saddest prelude, providing a peculiar sort of divertissement. I was amused by the way his wig and glue-on mustache stumbled with the movements of his performance. But I couldn't laugh when I looked at those hands with their long, translucent fingernails caressing the keys without breaking.

What I saw was distracting. I had no interest in being hypnotized by his eccentric character and that melancholy music. When I lowered my head, I was reminded of that other exceedingly strange detail—the marble floor was flecked with countless drains, distributed throughout the living room.

Outside it began to rain. I heard drops hitting the covered windows. Nervous, I sat up and granted myself permission to stroll through the house while listening to the Count playing piano. I meandered from the living room to the dining room that had once overlooked the ravine. Here too the windows were blocked off. In their place, a long painted mural of a landscape—using the technique of trompe l'oeil to trick a viewer into seeing a three-dimensional reality—stretched across the length of the wall. An ancient castle arose in the middle of a desolate countryside, where birds of prey circled a dry forest and a wasteland occupied by wolves. On the castle's terrace, minutely depicted, a woman and a little girl stood, terrified and imploring.

I had thought there wouldn't be any paintings in this house.

I shook my head to shoo away the image.

Then I took the liberty of interrupting Count Vlad.

"Count, Sir, I just need you to sign these documents. If you don't mind, could you to do it now? It's getting late, and I'm expected for dinner."

I held out the papers and a pen to the tenant. He sat up, adjusting his ridiculous wig.

"How fortunate!" he said. "You have a family."

"Yes," I stammered. "My wife was the one who found this house for you."

"Ah! I hope she'll come visit me one of these days."

"She is very busy, you know, with her business."

"Ah! But I'm sure that she knew this house before I did,

Mr. Navarro. She walked through these hallways. She stood in this living room . . ."

"Of course, yes, of course . . ."

"Tell her she left her scent behind."

"Say again?"

"Yes, tell—is her name Asunción? Asunción, that's what my friend Zurinaga told me she's called. Like the Feast of the *Asunción*? The Assumption? . . . Tell Asunción that her scent still lingers, suspended in the air of this house."

"Why not? Your gallantry—"

"Tell your wife that I am breathing her scent . . ."

"Yes, I will. How very gallant," I said. "Now, if you'll please excuse me, good night. And enjoy your stay."

"I have a ten-year-old daughter. You do, too, don't you?"

"Yes, Count, that's right."

"I hope that they'll meet and like each other. Bring her around, so she can play with Minea."

"Minea?"

"My daughter, Mr. Navarro. Let Borgo know."

"Borgo?"

"My servant."

Vlad snapped his fingers, which made the sound of a rattle and a castanet. His glass fingernails shone. Then a small, twisted man appeared, a small hunchback with the most beautiful face that I have ever seen on a man. He was a sculptural vision, one of those ideal profiles from ancient Greece, like Cellini's *Perseus*. Borgo's was a face of perfect symmetry brutally set above a deformed body, both disparate aspects united by his long mane of feminine, honey-colored curls. His expression was sad, ironic, and coarse.

"At your service, *monsieur*," said the servant, in French, with a distant accent.

I hurried my goodbyes, trying not to be rude but without success: "I believe everything is in order. I suppose we won't be seeing each other again. Enjoy your stay. Thank you . . . I mean, goodnight." I regretted, in an instant, having offended my client.

I could not parse, beyond so many layers of disguises, his look of disdain, scorn, and glee. I could superimpose onto Count Vlad any expression that I chose. He wore a mask. Borgo the servant, on the contrary, had nothing to hide, and I admit that his transparency frightened me more than the truculence of the Count, who bade me good-bye as though I had not said a word.

"Don't forget. Tell your wife—Asunción, right?—that your little girl is always welcome."

Borgo brought a candle near his master's face and added, "We could play together, the three of us."

He cackled and slammed the door in my face.

5

On a storm-filled night like this, the boundary between dream and life becomes porous. Asunción sleeps beside me after a round of intense sex, that I urged, all but imposed, aware that I needed to compensate for the mournful mood of my visit to the Count.

I do not intend to repeat what I already said about my love life with Asunción, and in any case discretion restrains my descriptions. But tonight, as if my will—to say nothing of my words—did not belong to me, I surrendered to such intense erotic pleasure that, as the afterglow fades, I find myself wondering if I've forgotten anything.

The tried-and-false question that a man puts to a woman—"Was it good for you, baby?"—soon becomes ridiculous. She will always say yes, first with words, and later with a nod, but if, after a while, we still insist on an answer, the *yes* will be tinged with the hiss of irritation. I now ask myself the same question. Did I satisfy her? Did I give her all the pleasure that she deserves? I know that I was satisfied, sure, but to be so selfish as to consider only my own pleasure would degrade me and would degrade my wife. They say that a woman can fake an orgasm, but that a man cannot. I believe that a man only obtains as much pleasure as he gives to a woman. Asunción, I wonder, does the pleasure that I have and that I give to you, which satisfies me, also fulfill you? Because I cannot ask her again, I must deduce the answer, take the temperature of her skin, detect the rhythm of her moans, gauge the force of her orgasms. I must contemplate her, take reckless pleasure in rediscovering her sex, the depth of the occluded spring of her navel, the maypoles that are her erect nipples in the midst of the sweet, pillowy, maternal softness of her breasts, her long neck out of a Modigliani, her face covered by the bend of her arm, the suggestive angle of her open legs, her pale thighs, her ugly feet, the delicious quivering of her rear-end . . . I see and I feel all these things, my beloved Asunción, and since I can no longer ask if it was good for you, I am left with the certainty of my own pleasure and the profound, inexplicable uncertainty of yours. Did she like it? Was it as good for you as it was for me, my one and only? Is there something you desire that you're not asking me for? Is there a final trace of modesty that prevents you from asking for something kinkier than we've done so far, a dirtier word?

Then I think of the palpitating sensation of Asunción's body. I notice the contrast between her long, black, lustrous, straight hair and the grimace of her genitals, the wild tangle of her short hair, crouched like a panther, indomitable like a bat, that forces me to flee, to penetrate her if only to save myself from her, to lose myself in her in order to conceal with my own pubic hair the wild jungle that grows in between Asunción's legs, ascending through the mound of Venus and then climbing the ivy along the womb, longing to graze the navel, that fountain of life . . .

I get out of bed tonight with the feeling that I forgot to say or to do something. How can I know what Asunción won't tell me? And how is she going to tell me if she closes her eyes when we finish and is silent? She doesn't even allow me to get a glimpse of whether she's really satisfied, or if she desires more—whether for the sake of our shared life, she's keeping a predilection to herself merely because she knows my shortcomings all too well?

I kiss her again, as if expecting that, from our joined lips, the truth of who we are and what we want might be given voice.

I watch her sleep for a long time in the early morning.

Then, extending my hand under the bed, I feel around for my slippers.

I always leave them there, but now I can't find them.

I stretch my arm further under the bed. I pat around then retract my hand in horror.

I touch, my hand touches, another hand, a hand under the bed.

The cold hand has long, smooth, and glassy fingernails.

I take a deep breath and close my eyes.

I sit up on the edge of the bed, and put my feet on the carpet.

I steel myself to begin my daily routine.

Then I feel that frozen hand grab me tight by the ankle, dig the glass fingernails into the soles of my feet. I hear a whisper in a deep voice:

"Sleep. Sleep. It's still too early. Go back to bed. There's no rush. Sleep, sleep."

Then I have the feeling that someone has left the room.

6

In my dream someone had been in my bedroom but then that someone walked out of it. From then on, the bedroom was no longer mine. It became a strange room because someone had walked out.

I woke with a start from the nightmare. I looked at the clock with disbelief. It was noon. I touched my temples. I rubbed my eyes. I was overcome by a feeling of guilt. I was late for work. I had failed in my duty. I hadn't even called in with an excuse.

I grabbed the phone and instead called Asunción at her office.

When I explained, she laughed in a singsong way and said, "Darling, I totally understand why you're tired."

"Aren't you tired, too?" I said, trying to match her levity.

"Hmmm, *you* were the one who did all the heavy lifting last night. What on earth got into you? For now just take it easy. Try to get some rest. You deserve it, my love," she said. "Oh and thanks for everything."

"You want to know something?"

"What?"

"Last night, when we were making love, I had this feeling like someone was watching us."

"Excellent," she said, then explained. "It was so good, I hope they're jealous."

I asked about our daughter. Asunción told me that today was a holiday at the Catholic school. "The Feast of the Assumption of the Virgin Mary, her ascent to heaven just as she was in life: not a legal holiday. And since it's the same day as Chepina's birthday—you remember Chepina, Josefina Alcayaga, the daughter of Alcayaga the engineer and his wife María de Lourdes?—there's a party for the kids, and I took Magdalena there early, so while I was there I collected the engineer's invoices for the tunnel that he custom built at your client's house, the Count . . ."

Guilt had my tongue until I made the connection and announced, "*Asunción*. If today's the Feast of the *Assumption*, then it's your Saint's Day."

"Well, you and I don't follow the religious calendar . . ."

"Asunción, today's your Saint's Day."

"Of course it is. Knock it off."

"Sorry, love."

"Yves, sorry for what?"

"I didn't congratulate you in time."

"Don't be silly. Think about last night's celebration. Listen, I was sure that that was your way of celebrating with me. And it was. And I thank you."

I listened to her quiet laugh.

"Okay, darling. Everything's in order," Asunción concluded. "I'll pick up our little girl this afternoon, and we'll see each other at dinner. And if you want, later we can celebrate the Assumption of the Holy Mother, the Virgin Mary, again."

She laughed again, flirtatiously this time, while preserving the professional tone of voice that she automatically adopts at the office.

"Get some rest. You deserve it. Bye."

I had barely hung up when the phone rang. It was Zurinaga.

"You were on the phone for a long time, Navarro," he said impatiently, not in keeping with his habitual courtesy. "I've been trying to reach you for hours."

"Ten minutes at the most, Sir," I replied firmly and without further explanation.

"I'm sorry, Yves," he said returning to his normal tone. "It's just that I need to ask you a favor."

"My pleasure, Don Eloy."

"It's urgent. You must go to Count Vlad tonight."

"Why doesn't he call me himself?" I said, trying to imply to him that being an "errand boy" was in keeping neither with Don Eloy Zurinaga's character nor my own.

"They still haven't installed his phone."

"And how did he get in touch with you?" I asked, now, a bit annoyed. I was still filthy and sticky from lovemaking. My cheeks were pocked with stubble. Sweat had collected uncomfortably in my armpits, and there was a tickling sensation on my curly-haired head.

"He sent his servant."

"Borgo?" I asked.

"Yes—why, have you seen him?"

He did not say *meet*. He said *see*.

The famous Count did not have, not by a long shot, the charm and grace of the Gypsy. I reminded myself that I had sworn never to return to Count Vlad's house. The business was settled. Besides, I needed to show my face at the office, if only to keep up appearances. The absence of Zurinaga, the senior partner, was bad enough. If I, the second in command, were absent too, it would be asking for trouble.

"I'm going to swing by the office, Don Eloy," I said firmly, instead of answering his peculiar question about Borgo, "and later I'll stop by to see the client."

Without saying a word, Zurinaga hung up the phone.

I was on my way to work, driving on the Periférico, the ring road around Mexico City. I inched my BMW through traffic at the pace of a tortoise on a mission.

I was worried to death about Magdalena, who was over at the Alcayagas' house. But I felt a little better when I remembered that Asunción had said, "Don't worry, dear. I'll pick her up, and we'll see each other at dinner."

"So what time are you picking her up?" I'd asked.

"You know how children's parties are; they go on forever. And María de Lourdes has enough activities scheduled to go on for weeks. There's tag, hide and seek, you're it! And, let me tell you, María has an arsenal of piñatas and goody bags stuffed with whistles and flutes. And there'll be enough punch and cake to feed an army of children."

She'd laughed as she finished. "Don't you remember? Even you were once a child."

7

The hunchback opened the door and brought his face much too close to mine, staring at me insolently. His breath reeked of yogurt. When he finally recognized me, he gave a fawning bow.

"Come in, Licenciado Navarro. My master is expecting you."

I entered and searched in vain for the Count in the large living room.

"Waiting where?"

"Go on upstairs to the bedroom."

I climbed a semicircular staircase that had no banister. The servant remained at the foot of the stairs. I don't know whether he was overdoing a show of courtesy or of subservience, or whether he was just observing me with suspicion. On the upper floor, all the doors to what I reckoned were bedrooms were shut, except for one. I approached that one and entered a room with a wide bed. By that time it was already nine o'clock at night, but I noticed that the bed was still covered with black satin, and had not been turned down for the master to retire for the evening.

There were no mirrors in the room, but below where a mirror might have hung stood a vanity with all sorts of cosmetics, and a row of wig stands. While he combed his wig and applied his makeup, it seemed, the Count would have to imagine himself.

A light steam billowed from an open bathroom door. I hesitated for a moment; I felt as though I must be invading my client's privacy . . . But he said from within, "Come in, Mr. Navarro, come on in. Don't be shy . . ."

In the bathroom, the steam emanating from the shower filled the air. Count Vlad was washing himself behind a dripping lacquer door. I looked away. Still, curiosity got the better of me. Through the fog, I noticed that the bathroom too lacked mirrors. The bathroom also lacked the usual tools of hygiene: shaving brush, comb, razor, toothbrush, toothpaste . . . As in the rest of the house, there were drains in every corner.

Vlad opened the door and emerged from the shower,

showing himself naked before my discomfited gaze.

He had shed his wig and his mustache.

His body was as white as plaster.

He did not have a single hair anywhere—not on his head, not on his chin, not on his chest, not in his armpits, not around his genitals, and not on his legs.

He was totally smooth, like an egg.

Or a skeleton.

He looked as though he'd been flayed.

But his face was still wrinkled like a pale lemon, and his gaze remained hidden by those dark glasses that were almost like a mask, stuck on his olive-colored sockets and fitted on his tiny ears sown with scars.

"Ah, Mr. Navarro," he said with a wide, red smile. "At last we see each other as we really are . . ."

Standing next to a naked Central European count who liked to discuss the philosophy of life and death, I tried to lighten things up a little.

"Sorry, Sir, Count," I said. "But I'm fully dressed."

"How can you be so sure?" he asked. "Doesn't fashion enslave and undress us all?"

At the edges of his affable smile, now without the fake-mustache disguise, two sharp canines glinted, yellow like the lemon color suggested by the pallor of his face when observed from up close.

"Excuse my indiscretion. Please, hand me my robe. It's hanging over there," the Count said as he pointed into the distance. "Let's go downstairs," he said hastily, "for dinner."

"Pardon me. I have dinner plans with my family."

"Your wife?"

"Yes. That's right."

"Your daughter?"

I nodded. He let out a cartoonish laugh.

"It's 9 P.M.," he deadpanned. "Do you know where your children are?"

I thought of Didier, who was dead, and of Magdalena who had gone to Chepina's birthday party and who should be back home by now while I remained here like an idiot in the bedroom of a naked, hairless, grotesque old man who was asking me at 9 P.M. if I knew where my children were.

I ignored his creepiness, confused.

"May I call home?" I asked.

Zurinaga had warned me. I had taken the precaution of bringing my cell phone. I took it out of my pants pocket and speed-dialed my house. I brought my hand up to my head. There was no answer. I heard my own voice tell me to "Leave a message." Something kept me from speaking, a feeling of uselessness, of a lack of freedom, of being dragged against my will down a slope like the one that plunged behind this house into the domain of pure uncertainty, a realm without free will . . .

"They must still be at the Alcayagas'," I muttered to reassure myself.

"The Alcayagas? You mean the kind engineer who designed and built the tunnel behind this house?"

"Yes," I said in a fog, and not just the one produced by the steam still billowing from the bathroom, "that's him—that's his family and him."

I selected their number and pushed TALK.

"Hello, María de Lourdes?"

"Yes?"

"It's Yves, Yves Navarro . . . Magdalena's father . . ."

"Oh, yes, how are you, Yves?"

"My daughter . . . No one's answering the phone at our house."

"Don't worry. Magdalena's sleeping over here. Chepina's having a sleepover."

"May I speak with her?"

"Yves, don't be cruel. They were exhausted. They went down an hour ago . . ."

"But my wife, Asunción . . ."

"She didn't show. She never came for Magdalena, but she called. She said she was running late at the office and would go straight to meet you at your mutual client's house—what's his name?"

"Count Vlad."

"That's it, Count What's-his-name. Foreign names are so hard for me to pronounce! And she said you should wait for her there."

"But, how'd she know I'd be coming here?"

María de Lourdes hung up. Vlad gave me a sarcastic look. He feigned a shiver.

"Yves . . . is it alright if I call you by your first name?"

I nodded without thinking.

"And remember, all my friends call me Vlad. Yves, my robe please. Do you want me to catch pneumonia? There, in the armoire, the one on the left."

I approached the closet like a sleepwalker. I opened the door to find there was only a single garment in the closet, an old heavy brocade robe, a bit threadbare, its collar made of wolf fur. It was a long robe that reached down to the ankles, worthy of a czar from a Russian opera, and embroidered in antique golds.

I took the garment and tossed it over Count Vlad's shoulders.

"Yves," the Count said, "don't forget to close the armoire door."

I looked back at the *closet* (a word obviously unknown to Vlad Radu) and only then did I see, stuck with thumbtacks to the inside of the door, a photograph of my wife, Asunción, with our daughter, Magdalena, sitting on her mother's lap.

"Vlad. Call me Vlad. All my friends call me Vlad."

8

I have no idea what possessed me that night, but against my better judgment, I stayed for dinner with Vlad. At best I can rationalize why I didn't return home. There was nothing to worry about. My daughter, Magdalena, was fine, sleeping over at the Alcayagas'. My wife, Asunción, was simply running late; she would come for me right here at Count Vlad's, and I would drive her home. In any case I called my wife's cell phone, and when she didn't answer, left the usual message.

I didn't mention having discovered the photograph. Such an acknowledgment would give this suspect individual the upper hand. The only defenses I had against him were to keep calm, to ask for no explanations, and to never seem surprised. What else could a good lawyer do? Zurinaga must have given pictures of me, of my family, to the exiled Balkan nobleman, so that he could see with whom he would be dealing in this faraway and exotic country, Mexico.

That explanation calmed my nerves.

The Count and I sat at either end of a strange, opaque, non-reflective lead table, unlikely to stimulate one's appetite, especially if the meal—as this one—consisted only of animal organs. Livers, kidneys, testicles, stomachs, and slack skins . . . were all smothered in sauces of onions and herbs that I recognized thanks to the old French recipes that my mother enjoyed: parsley, tarragon, of course, and others whose taste I did not recognize—but my mother had always used garlic as well.

So I asked, "You have any garlic?" expecting a withering look and sudden silence, followed by a swift change of subject.

"We use pork dust, Maître Navarro. From an old recipe that Saint Eutychius prescribed to expel a demon that a nun had swallowed up without noticing."

Vlad seemed amused by my look of skepticism.

"According to a well-known legend in my country," Count Vlad continued, "the unsuspecting nun sat herself directly over the devil, so he defended his action as follows: 'What else could I do? She squatted over a bush, and the bush was me . . .'"

I concealed my disgust well.

"*Les entrées et les sorties*, Maître Navarro. That's what life comes down to: *entrances and exits*; it sounds better in this barbaric tongue. From the front and from the rear. What goes in must come out; what comes out must go in. The habits of hunger vary. What one culture finds disgusting is a delicacy to another. Imagine what the French think of Mexicans eating ants and grasshoppers and worms. But don't the French gourmets themselves savor frogs and snails? Show me an Englishman who appreciates *mole poblano*; his stomach turns at the thought of that mixture of chili, chicken, and chocolate . . . And don't you adore *huitlacoche, common smut* to the botanist, the fungus that grows on corn, which so disgusts the rest of the world that they would only feed it to their pigs? And speaking of pigs, how can the English stand their dishes cooked—or rather ruined—in lard, which is pig fat? Not to mention the North Americans, who so lack any sense of taste that eating newsprint would make them lick their chops in delight."

He laughed in that characteristic way of his, forcibly lowering his upper lip as if he wanted to hide his intentions.

"You have to be like the wolf, Mr. Navarro. We can observe such wisdom in the old Latin *lupus*, my Teutonic *wulfaz*. We find natural and eternal wisdom in wolves—harmless in the summer and in the fall, when they are sated—who only hunt when they're hungry, in the winter and in the spring! When they are hungry . . ."

He made a commanding gesture with his pale hand, intensified by its glazed nails.

The role of the butler was assumed by Borgo the hunchback, and serving the dishes was a slow-moving maid, pointlessly urged on by the snapping fingers of Borgo, who wore for the occasion a little red-and-black-striped jacket and a bow tie, a costume generally only seen in old French movies. He thought that by wearing this old-fashioned uniform, he could, coquettishly, make up for his physical deformity. At least that's what I understood from his satisfied and (sometimes) suggestive glances.

"I am deeply grateful to you for accepting my invitation, Maître Navarro. I usually eat alone and, *croyez moi*, that gives me very sad thoughts."

The servant poured me some red wine, but offered none to his master. I shot Vlad a quizzical look as I raised my glass to propose a toast . . .

"I told you . . ." the Count said, staring at me with good-natured mockery.

"Yes, you don't drink wine," I said, trying to keep things light and friendly. "Do you drink alone?"

Following his habit of ignoring what had just been said and then continuing on some other subject, Vlad just said, "Telling the truth is unbearable to mortals."

I let myself be a little rude and pressed him for an answer. "It was a simple question. Do you drink alone?"

"Telling the truth is unbearable to mortals."

"I don't know about that. I'm mortal and I'm a lawyer. That sounds like one of those syllogisms they teach us at school. All men are mortal. Socrates is a man. Therefore, Socrates is mortal."

"Children don't lie," he went on, ignoring me. "And they can be immortal."

"Say what?"

A woman's hands in black gloves offered me the platter of organ meat. I felt revulsion, but my manners required that I take a bit of liver from here and a bit of tripe from there . . .

"Thank you."

The woman who served me moved with a light rustling of skirts. I had not lifted my eyes, busy as I was choosing the least disgusting available meats. I smiled at my own discomfort. Who looks at a waiter's face while he's serving us, anyway? I saw her walk away, from behind, with the platter in hand.

"That's why I love children," Vlad said, not touching his food but inviting me to eat with a gesture of his hand and those long, glassy fingernails. "You know, a child is like a small, unfinished God."

"An unfinished god?" I asked, surprised. "Wouldn't that be a better definition of the devil?"

"No, the devil is a fallen angel."

I took a gulp of wine to steel myself for a long, unwelcome exchange of abstract ideas with my host. Why hadn't my wife come to my rescue yet?

"Yes," Vlad said, resuming his discourse. "The abyss in God's understanding is his awareness that he is still unfinished. But if God were finished, his creation would end with him. The world cannot be the simple legacy of a dead God. Ha, a retired God, collecting a pension. Imagine the world as a circle of corpses, a heap of ashes . . . No, the world must be the endless work of an unfinished God."

"What does any of that have to do with children?" I muttered, realizing as I spoke that I was a little tongue-tied.

"I believe that children are the unfinished part of God. God needs the secret life force of children in order to continue to exist."

"I, ah . . ." I muttered with a voice now faint.

"You don't want to sentence children to old age, do you Mr. Navarro?"

I protested with a helpless gesture, slamming my hand down, spilling the remnant of my wine on the lead table.

"I lost a son, you old bastard . . ."

"To abandon a child to old age," the Count repeated impassively, "to old age. And to death."

Borgo picked up my glass. My head fell to the metal table.

Just as I lost consciousness, I heard Count Vlad continue, "Didn't the Unmentionable One say, 'Suffer the little children, and forbid them not to come unto me'?"

9

I woke with a start. I didn't know where I was. This displaced feeling was one I'd experienced before on long trips. I didn't recognize the bed or the large room in which I found myself. When I checked my watch, it was twelve o'clock. But was it noon or midnight? My head pounded. Heavy baize curtains covered the windows. I stood, and when I pulled back the curtains found myself staring into a brick wall. This brought me to my senses. I was, I realized, in Count Vlad's house. All his windows had been walled off. From inside the house, there was no way to distinguish day from night.

I was still dressed in the same clothes as at that execrable dinner. So what had happened? The Count and his servant had drugged me. Or was it that invisible woman? Asunción must never have come to rescue me, as she had promised. Magdalena would still be at the Alcayagas' house. No, if it were noon, she'd be at school. Today wasn't a holiday. The feast of the Assumption of the Virgin had concluded. The two girls, Magdalena and Chepina, were together at school, safe.

My head was a maelstrom, and the profusion of drains in the Count's house made my body feel like a liquid that was losing its shape, flowing away, spilling into the ravine . . .

The *ravine*.

Sometimes one word, just one word, gives us an answer, restores our reason, or inspires action. And more than anything, I needed to think and to act: not to rehash how I ended up in this absurd and inexplicable situation, but to get out of it as soon as possible. I was sure that, if I escaped, I would understand everything later.

With a natural and reflexive gesture, I touched my chin and cheeks. Rubbing the stubble of my growing beard, I could tell that about twenty-four hours had elapsed since I'd last shaved . . . so I knew that the dinner had taken place "the night before" and that now was "the day after." I ran my impatient hands over my wrinkled suit, my smelly shirt, and my mussed hair. I tried to straighten the knot of my tie. I did all this as I walked out of the bedroom on the top floor of the house and opened the doors to the other bedrooms, one after the other, taking note of the fact that each room was in perfect order, with perfectly made beds, and in each one discovering no sign that anyone had spent the night there. Unless, I reasoned—and was grateful that my erstwhile sense of logic had returned from its long nocturnal exile—unless everyone had gone out, and the industrious Borgo had already made the beds . . .

One bedroom caught my attention. I was drawn to it by a distant melody, which I recognized as the French lullaby, "Frère Jacques."

> *Frère Jacques, Frère Jacques*
> *Dormez-vous? Dormez-vous?*
> *Sonnez les matines! Sonnez les matines!*
> *Ding-dang-dong. Ding-dang-dong.*

I walked into the room and approached a chest of drawers. A small music box was playing the little song, while a little shepherdess, dressed in an eighteenth-century style, holding a hooked staff, and with a lamb next to her, turned in circles.

Here everything was pink: the curtains, the backs of the chairs, the nightdress carefully laid out next to the pink pillow. The short, little girl's nightie trailed ribbons from its embroidered hem. There was a pair of pink slippers too. No mirrors. A perfect but unoccupied room. It was a room that was waiting for someone. There was only one thing missing: there were no flowers here. And all of a sudden I noticed that there were half a dozen dolls reclining against the pillows. They were all blonde and all dressed in pink. But none of them had legs.

I left the room refusing to allow myself to think about it, and I went to the Count's bedroom. The wigs were still there, on their wig stands, as though warning of the presence of some otherworldly guillotine. The bathroom was dry. The bed, untouched.

I went downstairs to silent sitting rooms. There was a faint smell of mold. I continued through the impeccably clean dining room. I entered the kitchen, messy and nasty smelling, clouded by the steam coming off heaps of entrails strewn across the floor, and from the remains of a huge, indescribable animal I could not identify, drawn and quartered on the tiled table. Beheaded.

The blood of the beast was still running into the drains on the kitchen floor.

I covered my mouth and nose in horror. I wanted to prevent even a single trace of the miasma rising off of this butchery from entering my body. Taking small steps backward, half-fearing that the animal would come back from the dead to attack me, I bumped up against some kind of leather curtain that gave way when I leaned against it. I drew the curtain aside. It was the entrance to a tunnel.

I recalled Vlad's insistence on having a passage connecting his house with the ravine. It was too late to turn back. I entered, groping the dark space between the walls. I moved with extreme caution, unsure of what I was doing, looking for a way out, some guiding light in the dark tunnel, with no luck, allowing myself to be guided solely by my subconscious, which impelled me to explore every inch of Vlad's mansion.

It was too dark. I reached for my cigarette lighter. I lit it and saw what I feared, what I should have known I would see. Unadulterated horror. The heart of the mystery.

Coffins and more coffins, there were at least a dozen coffins lined up along the tunnel's length.

The impulse to turn tail and run from that place was strong, but not as strong as my will to know, my foolish and detestable curiosity, my investigative lawyer's reflexes, as I opened coffin after coffin in a fit of self-loathing, unable to find anything but earth inside each one, until I opened the coffin in which my client, Count Vlad Radu, lay in perfect peace, dressed in his turtleneck shirt, his pants, and his black moccasins, with his glass-fingernailed hands crossed over his chest and his bald head resting on a small red silk pillow, as red as the cushioned interior of the box.

I stared at him intensely, unable to wake him and demand an explanation, paralyzed by the terror of this encounter, hypnotized by the details I was only now discovering, having Vlad before me, prostrate, at my mercy, but I was clueless, after all, about which actions I could take, under the sway, as I was, of the legend of the vampire, the tactics recommended by superstition and science, in this case indistinguishable. The garlic necklace, the cross, the stake . . .

The intense cold in the tunnel drew fog from my open mouth, but it also cleared my head and allowed me to observe closely certain phenomena: Vlad's ears—too small, and surrounded by scars, which I attributed to a series of facial surgeries—had grown overnight. I saw them struggle to spread out like the wings of a sinister bat. What did this damned creature do—trim his ears every evening before going out into the world in order to disguise his resemblance to a nocturnal chiropter?

A drop of some horrid liquid splattered on my head. I lifted my gaze. Bats hung upside down, holding on to the tunnel's rock ceiling by their claws.

An unbearable stench emerged from the corners of Vlad's coffin, where bat guano—vampire shit—had collected . . .

Vampire shit. Count Vlad's ears. The phalanx of blind rats hanging over my head. These were insignificant compared to the most sinister detail.

Vlad's eyes.

Vlad's eyes without his dark, ever-present sunglasses.

Two empty sockets.

Two eyes without eyes.

Two lagoons incarnate with crimson shores and depths of black blood.

That's when the realization finally sank in. Vlad did not have eyes. His black sunglasses were his real eyes. They allowed him to see.

I don't know what affected me the most when I quickly shut the lid of the coffin in which Count Vlad slept.

I don't know if it was the horror itself.

I do not know if it was the surprise, or my lacking the tools to destroy him right then and there—my empty, vulnerable hands.

No. I do know.

I know that it was my concern over my wife, Asunción, and my daughter, Magdalena. I had a suspicion, one that would be rejected by daylight logic, that something might have united Vlad's destiny to that of my family . . . and if that was the case, I had no right to touch anything, to disturb the mortal peace of the monster.

I tried to recover the normal rhythm of my breathing. My heart pounded with fear. But when I breathed, I noticed the real smell of this catacomb built for Count Vlad, the smell beneath the ammoniacal stench of batshit. It wasn't a smell that I recognized. I tried but couldn't associate it with scents I knew. This smell that permeated the tunnel was not only distinct from any other scent that I had ever smelled, was not only different . . . it was a stench that came from somewhere else entirely. From a faraway place.

10

I made it home just before one o'clock in the afternoon. At my house in the El Pedregal neighborhood of San Ángel, our maid, Candelaria, welcomed me in great distress.

"Oh, Señor! I was terrified! That was the first time nobody came home at night! I was all alone."

What? Had my wife not returned? Where had our daughter gone?

I telephoned Mrs. Alcayaga.

"How are you, Yves? Yes, Magdalena went to school with Chepina very early this morning. No, nothing to worry about. She's such a tidy little girl and cuter than a button. I ironed her clothes myself while she took a shower. At the school, I explained that Magdita wouldn't be in uniform today because she wound up sleeping over the night before. Okay, see ya, bye."

I phoned Asunción's office. "No," her secretary said, "she hasn't been here since yesterday. Is something the matter?"

I showered, shaved, and changed my clothes.

"Don't you want your chilaquiles, Señor?" asked Candelaria. "Your coffee?"

"Thanks, Candelaria, but I'm in a big hurry. If my wife shows up, tell her to stay put and wait for me."

I looked around the living room out of the unbreakable habit of checking that everything was in order before going out. We notice nothing when everything is in its place. We feel at ease when we go out. Nothing is out of place; habit reassures us ...

There were no flowers in the house. The bouquets habitually arranged with such care and joy by Asunción, in the vestibule, in the living and dining rooms, visible from where I stood about to go out, were not there. There were no flowers in the house.

So I asked, "Candelaria, why aren't there any flowers?"

The maid's face looked grave. Her eyes staunched a reproach.

"The Señora threw them in the trash, Señor. Before going out yesterday, she said, 'They're all dried out, I forgot to put them in water. Throw them out already ...'"

The crystalline afternoon surprised me. Our valley of sickly haze, once a place of such clear air, had recovered its high visibility and its gorgeous cumulus clouds. This scene restored the mettle that the recent series of unsettling and strange events had snatched away from me.

I drove fast but carefully. Despite everything that had happened, my good habits came back to me, and those habits reinforced my reason. I longed for the city as it used to be, back when the capital was small, safe, walkable, breathable, crowned with awe-inspiring clouds, and encircled by mountains cut out with scissors . . .

Soon, I was disconcerted again.

"No," the school principal said, "Magdalena is absent today."

"But her classmates, her little friends, can I speak with them, with Chepina?"

No, the girls had not seen Magdalena at any party yesterday.

"At your party, Chepina."

"There was no party, sir."

"It was your birthday."

"No, sir, my saint's day falls on the day of the Virgin."

"Of the Assumption, yesterday?"

"No sir, the Feast of the Annunciation to the Blessed Virgin Mary, that's my saint's day, but that's still a long way off."

The girl looked at me with impatience. I had come during her class's recess and was stealing precious minutes of her free time. Her baffled friends stared at Chepina.

I called Chepina's mother right away. I complained bitterly. Why had she lied to me?

"Please," she said in a tremulous voice, "don't ask me anything. Please, Mr. Navarro, I am begging for my life."

"What about my daughter's life? My daughter?" I demanded, practically screaming, and then repeating my words to myself after I violently cut off the call.

I jumped in my car and drove as fast as I could to Eloy Zurinaga's house in the Roma neighborhood, my last resort.

I had never before been so tortured by the slowness of the Mexico City traffic; the irritability of the drivers; the savagery of the dilapidated trucks that ought to have been banned ages ago; the sadness of begging mothers carrying children in their shawls and extending their callused hands; the awfulness of the crippled and the blind asking for alms; the melancholy of the children in clown costumes trying to entertain with their painted faces and the little balls they juggled; the insolence and obscene bungling of the pot-bellied police officers leaning against their motorcycles at strategic highway entrances and exits to collect their bite-size bribes; the insolent pathways cleared for the powerful people in their bulletproof limousines; the desperate, self-absorbed, and absent gaze of old people unsteadily crossing side streets without looking where they were going, those white-haired, nut-faced men and women resigned to die the same way as they lived; the giant billboards advertising an imaginary world of bras and underpants covering small swaths of perfect bodies with white skin and blonde hair, high-priced shops selling luxury and enchanted vacations in promised paradises.

I drove through long cement tunnels as sinister as the labyrinth built for Count Vlad by his vile lackey, the engineer Alcayaga, husband of the no less vile and deceitful María de Lourdes, mother of the sweet but impatient little girl Chepina, whom I began to imagine as yet another monster, an oozing snot-faced young succubus . . .

I braked hard in front of the house of my boss, Don Eloy Zurinaga. A manservant with nondescript features opened the door and tried to block my way without anticipating my resolve, my increased strength in the face of uncertainty, born from the lies and the horror with which I confronted the elderly Zurinaga, seated as usual in front of the fireplace, his knees covered with a blanket, and his long white fingers caressing the worn leather of the armchair.

When he saw me, he opened his cloudy eyes, but the rest of his face was still. I paused, surprised by how much and how quickly the old man had aged. He was already old, but now he looked older still, as old as old age itself, because, as I suddenly perceived, this boss was no longer in charge, this man was defeated, his will had been obliterated by a force superior to his own. Eloy Zurinaga still breathed, but his corpse had already been hollowed by terror.

I was frightened to see what had become of a man who was my boss, to whom I owed a certain loyalty if not affection that he himself had never demanded of me, a man who had been above any attack on his indomitable personality. Whether he was honest or not, as I've already said, I did not know. But he was skillful, superior, and untouchable. This man had been the greatest expert in the cultivation of indifference that I'd ever met.

Not anymore. Now I stared at him sitting there with the shadows of the fire dancing on his pale face, the remains of a person bereft of beauty or virtue, a wretched old man. However, to my surprise, he still retained a few tricks, and even a bit of daring.

He raised his almost transparent hand. "I know. You figured out that the man with the polo coat and old Stetson whowent to the office was in fact me and not some double . . ."

I gave him a questioning look.

"Yes, that was me. The voice that called on the telephone to make you believe that it wasn't me, that I remained at home, was just a recording."

He smiled with difficulty.

"That's why I was so hurried on the phone. I couldn't allow any interruptions. I had to hang up quickly."

His old cunning shone again for an instant in his eyes.

"Why did I need to return twice to the office, Navarro, even though that entailed breaking the rule of my absence?"

He left a dramatic pause as though he expected me to answer this rhetorical question.

"Because, on both occasions, I had to consult old, forgotten papers that only I could find."

He spread his hands like someone who has solved a mystery and thus put an end to an investigation.

"I alone knew where they were. Pardon the mystery."

But he was no idiot. My eyes, my entire being, told him that this was not why I was visiting him today, and that I couldn't care less about his stupid tricks. But he was still a relentless lawyer who wouldn't admit to knowing anything until I told him myself.

"You have played with my life, Don Eloy, and with the lives of my loved ones. Believe me when I say that if you don't speak frankly with me, I won't be responsible for my actions."

He looked at me with the weakness of a wounded father, or a whipped dog. Suddenly he begged for mercy.

"If only you understood me, Yves."

I said nothing, but standing before him, defiant and angry, I didn't need to say anything. Zurinaga was defeated, not by me, by himself.

"He promised me eternal youth, immortality."

Zurinaga raised his vanquished eyes.

"We were the same, you see? When we met, we were the same, both of us young students, and in those days we aged at the same rate."

"And now, Counselor?"

"He came to see me the night before last. I thought it was to thank me for everything I had done for him, for arranging his move. I had answered his plea: 'I need fresh blood.' Oh!"

"So what happened?"

"He was no longer like me. He was young again. He laughed at me. He told me not to expect anything from him. I would never be young again. I had served him, like a menial, nothing more than a worn-out shoe. I would get older and die soon. He would be young forever, thanks to my naïve collaboration. He laughed at me. I was just one of his many servants. He said, 'I have the power to choose my age. I can look old, young, or even an age in keeping with the natural progress of time.'"

The lawyer clucked like a hen. He stared at me with the dying embers of his eyes, and he took my burning hand in his frozen one.

"Go back to Vlad's house, Navarro. This very night. Soon it will be too late."

I wanted to let go of his hand, but Eloy Zurinaga had concentrated in his fist all the strength of his deception, his disillusionment, his final breaths.

"Do you understand my predicament?"

"Yes, boss," I said almost sweetly, sensing his need for consolation, while feeling myself vulnerable because of my affection, memories, and even gratitude.

"You have to hurry. It's urgent. Have a look at these papers."

He let go of my hand. I took the papers he proffered and then walked toward the door. He said, as though from a great distance:

"From Vlad, you can expect nothing but evil."

And in a lower voice:

"Do you think I don't have scruples or even a conscience? Do you think I don't have a fever burning in my soul?"

I turned my back on him. I knew that I would never see him again.

11

In the year of Our Lord 1448, Vlad Tepes
ascended to the throne of Wallachia (having been invested earlier by Sigismund of
the House of Luxembourg, Holy Roman Emperor
of the German Nation), and he established
his capital at Targoviste, not far from
the Danube at the border of the Ottoman
Empire, tasked with the Christian mission
of fighting the Turk, into whose hands Vlad
fell, quickly learning the lessons of Sultan Murad II: strength alone sustains power,
and power requires the strength of cruelty.
Having escaped the Turks, Vlad recovered the
throne of Wallachia with a double ruse: the
Turks as well as the Christians believed him

to be their ally. But Vlad was only allied
with Vlad and with the power of cruelty itself. He burned down castles and villages
throughout Transylvania. He gathered all
the students who had come to study the local language in one room, and then he burned
them alive. He buried a man up to his navel
and then had him beheaded. Others he roasted
like pigs or slit their throats like lambs.
He captured the seven fortresses of Transylvania and ordered their inhabitants shredded
like lettuce. When the Gypsies were unwilling
to submit one of their own to hanging, because the practice was opposed by Tigani custom, Vlad forced them to boil the Gyspy alive
and then to feast on his flesh. One of Vlad's
lovers claimed, so he wouldn't lose interest
in her, that she was pregnant: just to make
sure, he used his knife to slice open her
womb. In 1462 he occupied the city of Nicopo-
lis and ordered the prisoners nailed down by
their hair until they died of starvation. He
beheaded the lords of Fogaras, cooked their

heads, and served them to the commoners. In
the village of Amlas, he cut off the breasts
of the women and forced their husbands to eat
them. In the capital, he gathered all the
poor, the sick, and the elderly of the region
to his palace; he wined and dined them and
asked them if they wished for anything else.

"No," they said, "we are satisfied."

So that they could die satisfied and never
again feel the need for anything, he had them
beheaded.

But he himself was not satisfied. He wanted
his name and deeds to live forever in history. Then he discovered a tool that would be
forever associated with him: the stake.

He captured the town of Beneşti and had all
its women and children impaled. He impaled
the boyars of Wallachia and the ambassadors
of Saxony. He impaled a captain who could
not bring himself to burn down the church of
Saint Bartholomew in Brasov. He impaled all
the merchants of Wuetzerland and appropriated
their property. He decapitated the children

of the village of Zeyding and then stuffed
the heads up their mothers' vaginas, and only
then did he impale the women. He liked to see
the impaled twitch and squirm on the stake
"like frogs." He had a donkey impaled on the
head of a Franciscan monk.

Vlad liked to cut off noses, ears, genitals, arms, and legs. Burn, boil, roast, cru-
cify, bury alive . . . He sopped up the blood
of his victims with his bread. When he became
more refined, he rubbed salt on his prisoners'
flayed feet before setting animals loose to
lick them.

But impaling people was his signature man-
ner of slaughter, and he took pleasure in all
the varieties of torture made possible by the
stake. The stake could penetrate the rectum,
the heart, or the navel. Thousands of men,
women, and children died on the stake during
the reign of Vlad the Impaler, though their
deaths could never quench his thirst for
power. His own death was the only one he saw
fit to impede.

He listened to the legends of his land with great desire, obsessed.

Legends of the muroni, capable of instant metamorphosis, turning themselves into cats, mastiffs, insects, spiders . . .

Of the nosferatu, hidden in the depths of forests, children of bastard parents, given over to wild orgies that exhaust them to death, although as soon as they are buried, the nosferatu awaken and abandon their graves, never again to return to them, and roam the night in the shape of black dogs, beetles, or butterflies. Poisoned by jealousy, they like to appear in nuptial chambers to render the newlyweds barren and impotent.

Of the lugosi, living corpses, given over to necrophilic orgies at gravesides, and who can be identified, and are often betrayed, by their chicken feet.

Of the strigoi of Braila who lie in their graves with their eyes perpetually open.

Of the varcolaci, with their pale faces and dry skin, who fall into a deep sleep and rise to the moon and devour it in their dreams: they were once children who died without being baptized.

This was the unyielding desire of Vlad the Impaler: to translate his cruel political power into cruel supernatural power; to rule not only over his time, but over eternity.

By 1457, Vlad the temporal monarch had provoked too many rivals to challenge his power: the local merchants and boyars, the warring dynasties and their respective supporters, the Habsburgs and their King Ladislaus the Posthumous, the Hungarian House of Hunyadi, and the Ottoman powers on the southern border of Wallachia. The latter declared themselves "enemies of Christ's Cross." The Christian kings associated Vlad with the religion of infidels. But the Ottomans, in turn, associated Vlad with the Holy Roman Empire and the Christian religion.

He was finally captured in battle by the faction run by the so-called Prince Basarab Laiota—a nimble ally, as is the Balkan practice, to all the powers at play, however hostile they were toward each other. Vlad the Impaler was condemned to be buried alive at an encampment next to the Tirnava River and was paraded along the route, heaped with scorn and derision, through crowds of the survivors of his infinite crimes, who—as Vlad was led past them in chains, standing on a cart, on his way to his burial ground—turned their backs on him. Nobody wanted to be on the receiving end of his final gaze.

Only one being was willing to face him. One person alone refused to turn her back on him. Vlad fixed his eyes on that creature who was but a little girl, a little girl who looked no older than ten. She stared at the Impaler with an impressive mixture of insolence and innocence, of tenderness and bitterness, of promise and despair.

Voivode, prince, Vlad the Impaler, Dracula—the name that all the inhabitants of Transylvania and Moldavia, Fogaras and Wallachia, the Carpathians and the Danube secretly

knew him by—was headed toward death-in-life,
dreaming of the living dead, the muroni, the
nosferatu, the strigoi, the varcolaci, the
vampires . . .

He was going to his death and was taking
with him only the blue gaze of a ten-year-old
girl, dressed in pink, the only one who neither
turned her back on him nor whispered, as the
others did, the Cursed Name of Dracula . . .

This, my dear Navarro, is a (partial) account
of the secrets that can be conveyed to you by
your loyal and reliable servant,

Eloy Zurinaga

12

While seated at the wheel of my parked BMW, I read Zurinaga's manuscript. Then I drove off. All possible feelings of disgust, astonishment, doubt, rebelliousness, and uncertainty had to be quarantined.

I drove robotically from the Roma neighborhood to the Chapultepec aqueduct within the backlit shadow of the eighteenth-century castle, and up on Paseo de la Reforma (formerly Paseo de la Emperatriz) on my way to Bosques de las Lomas. I was grateful that my habits allowed me to drive on autopilot, because I found myself lost in thought, given over to musings that were unusual for me, but that now seemed to focus my experience of these last few hours and seemed to arise spontaneously as the evening lights came on like blinking cat eyes along the route.

I was seized by an intense feeling of melancholy. Is the greatest moment of love, I wondered, a moment of sadness, uncertainty, and loss? Or rather, do we feel love at its most intense when it is right in front of our faces and thus less prone to be sacrificed to the foolishness of jealousy, of routine, of disrespect, or of negligence? I pictured my wife, Asunción, and recalling in an instant our entire relationship, our lives together, I said to myself that pleasure astonishes us: How is it possible, Asunción, that one's immortal soul can fuse with another's in a kiss and thus lose sight of the whole wide world?

I spoke to my beloved in this way because I didn't know what awaited me at the vampire's house. I repeated hopeful words to myself in the spirit of exorcism: love is always generous; it never loses heart because it is spurred on by a desire for total, infinite possession, and as this is not possible, we convert dissatisfaction into the spur of desire, and we embellish it, Asunción, with sadness, anxiety, and a celebration of the finite itself.

As if I foresaw what awaited me, Asunción, I let out a sob and said to myself:

"This is the greatest moment of our love."

Dusk had fallen when I arrived at Count Vlad's house. Borgo opened the door, and once again blocked my way. I was on the verge of striking the hunchback when he let me pass.

"The girl is out back," he said, "in the garden."

"What garden?" I asked, anxious and angry.

"What you call the ravine. The trees . . ." the servant indicated by pointing a slow finger.

Not betraying my panic, I walked through Vlad's mansion from the front door to the back to reach what Borgo called the garden but was instead a ravine with, as I recalled, a few dying willows grasping the slope of the land. Behind the house, I noticed, with astonishment, that all the trees had been chopped down and carved into stakes. Between two of these sharp poles hung a child's swing.

That's where I saw my daughter, Magdalena.

I ran to kiss her, unconcerned about everything around us.

"My girl, my little girl, my love," I cried. I kissed her, I hugged her, I caressed her curly hair and her burning cheeks, and I felt the fullness of the embrace that only a father and a daughter know how to share.

She moved away, smiling.

"Look, Daddy. This is my friend Minea."

I turned to see this other girl, the one called Minea, who took my Magdalena by the hand and drew her away from me. My little girl was dressed in her navy-blue school uniform with a white collar and a red bowtie.

The other girl was dressed all in pink, like the dolls that I had seen that morning in the pink bedroom. She wore a pink dress attached to a loose-fitting, frilly skirt with cloth roses sewn at the waist, pink stockings, and black patent-leather shoes. She had voluminous golden ringlets and tresses of corkscrew curls, with a huge pink bow crowning her head.

She was from another time. But she was identical to my daughter (who was also, as I mentioned, thanks to the influence of her mother, not exactly a modern girl).

The same height, the same face. Only their attire was different.

"What are you doing, Magda?" I said, suppressing my amazement.

"Look," she said, pointing at the stakes in the gully.

I saw nothing out of the ordinary.

"The squirrels, Daddy."

Yes, there were squirrels running up and down the trunks, scurrying nervously, and pausing to watch us, as though we were intruders, before they resumed their race.

"They're adorable, sweetheart. We have lots of them in the garden behind our house, you remember?"

Magdalena giggled, covering her mouth with a hand. She lifted the skirt of her school uniform while Minea did the same with her own skirt. Minea stuck her hand into the front of her own panties and took out a squirming squirrel, which she held tightly in her hands.

"Daddy, I bet you didn't know that squirrels' teeth grow inside until they pierce the top of their heads . . ."

My daughter took the squirrel that Minea offered to her and, lifting the skirt of her school uniform, she put the squirrel down her own panties, over her genitals.

I felt consumed by my horror. I had kept my gaze low, looking down at the girls without noticing Borgo's watchful proximity.

The servant approached my daughter and caressed her neck. I was revolted. Borgo laughed.

"Not to worry, Monsieur Navarro. My master doesn't allow me more than this. *Il se réserve les petits choux bien pour lui . . .*"

He spoke like a cook caressing a hen before cutting off its head. He let go of Magda, showing his empty hands in a plea for peace. In the slowly falling night of the plateau, it was becoming hard to make out what I was seeing in front of me.

"On the other hand, since Minea is part of the household . . ."

The lewd servant lifted the other girl's skirt and pulled up her pink ruffled dress until her face was covered, exposing her naked chest with its prepubescent nipples. Kneeling in front of Minea, he sucked on them.

"Oh, Monsieur Navarro!" he said, interrupting his filthy performance. "What shapely, budding nipples! What bliss!"

He moved his face away, and I saw that, on Minea's chest, the nipples had now disappeared.

I searched for my daughter's gaze, trying to divert her attention from these ghastly sights.

I don't know if I betrayed my disgust.

Magda's eyes seemed to say to me, "I hate you. You're embarrassing me. Leave me alone. I'm playing with my friend."

Go back to Vlad's house. Soon it will be too late.

Zurinaga's words resonated in that murky evening just beginning out there on the Mexican plateau, where hot days yield, in a split second, to cold nights.

13

Though that revolting display along the ravine sickened me, it did not divert me from my clear objectives: to confront the monster and to save my family. I did not abandon Magdalena, tempted as I was to flee.

Turning my back on Borgo, Minea, and my daughter, I located the entrance to the tunnel at the edge of the gully; I pushed open the metal door and entered the accursed Alcayaga's passageway, brand-new but already suffused with the mossy smell of centuries, as if—instead of having been constructed on site—it had been transported from the distant lands of Vlad Radu's native Wallachia.

Again that aroma, as though of sensually corrupt meats, sweetly rotting.

Tar and barnacles from ancient seas clung to the coffins. The smoky smell of sand that came from far away, from a land that was not my own, arose from creaky wooden planks and moldy nails.

I walked through the tunnel quickly, because I had already satisfied my curiosity about this lugubrious traveling cemetery—until I stopped and had to muffle a gasp. Vlad had appeared from behind a casket, blocking my way.

For a second, I didn't recognize him. He was wrapped in a mounted dragoon's cape, and black and lustrous hair fell to his shoulders. This wasn't just another wig. It was the hair of his youth—renewed, once again shiny and thick. I only recognized him by the shape of his face, by his chalky pallor, and by the black sunglasses that masked his bloody sockets.

I recalled Zurinaga's bitter quotation of Vlad's boast: he could choose his age at will, appear old, young, or even an age in keeping with the natural progress of time. He could fool us all . . .

"Where are you heading in such a hurry, Mr. Navarro?" he asked in his deep, slick voice.

That simple question threw me off my game. I had only left my daughter in the ravine so that I could confront Vlad. And here he was. But I had to give him another answer.

"I'm looking for my wife."

"Your wife doesn't interest me."

"That's good to know. I want to see her so that we can take Magdalena away with us. I'm not going to let you destroy our home."

Vlad smiled like a cat breakfasting on canaries.

"Navarro, let me explain the situation."

He turned with preternatural swiftness and opened a coffin, inside of which lay Asunción, my wife, pale and beautiful, dressed in black, with her hands crossed over her chest. I examined her neck, out of instinct. Two purple pricks, the tiniest bloody buds, bloomed above her jugular.

I was still trying to stifle my scream when Vlad moved behind me and with the strength of a gladiator smothered it himself with a spidery hand over my mouth, while his other hand grabbed me by the chest.

"Take a good look at her and listen carefully. I'm not interested in your wife, Navarro. I am interested in your daughter. She is the perfect companion for Minea. They're practically twins, did you notice? You should have seen the enormous quantity of photographs that I had to examine during the endless nights in my ruined castle in Wallachia until I found the girl who most closely resembled mine. And she was in Mexico, a city of twenty million new—as you might call them—victims! A city without police protection! You wouldn't believe the trouble Scotland Yard put me through in London! And, best of all—even though I have cultivated friendships all over the world—the city of my old—yes, elderly—friend Zurinaga! All served up on a silver platter, as it were . . . twenty million delectable blood sausages!"

Vlad showed his poor manners by licking his lips.

"They're practically twins, did you notice? Minea was the source of my life. You must believe in the true depths of my feelings, Navarro. You who know the mystical bonds that make a family. This girl is, in fact, my only true family."

He sighed sentimentally. As the Count loosened his grip over my body, I couldn't help but be fascinated by the creature's cynicism.

"With Minea, you see, I understood, I became aware of things I never knew. Imagine, my life, begun five centuries ago in the citadel of Sighişoara above the Târnava River, and in those days my life was all about fighting for political power, trying to secure the inheritance of my father, Vlad Dracul, fighting against my half-brother Alexandru for the throne of Wallachia, fighting against my father's lover Caktuna, who became a nun, just as my half-brother, her son, became a monk, both conspirators hiding behind the sanctity of the Church, fighting against the Turks who invaded my kingdom with the help of my traitorous and corrupt younger brother Radu, an ephebe of Sultan Mehmed's boys' harem—a prisoner myself of the Turks, Navarro, from whom I learned the most refined cruelties and from whom I escaped, armed with a vengeance that I unleashed until I dyed the Danube red, from Silistra to Tismana, filled the swamps of Balreni with corpses, blinded with iron and buried my enemies alive, and impaled on stakes all those who opposed my power, impaled them through the mouth, through the rectum, through the umbilicus: that's how I earned the title Vlad the Impaler. The papal nuncio Gabriele Rangone accused me of impaling a hundred thousand men and women, and the Pope himself condemned me to be buried incommunicado in the secret depths below an iron tombstone in a cemetery at the edge of the Târnava River after ruling that "consecrated ground will not receive your body," condemning me to remain forever unburied and yet buried alive . . . That is how the false legend of my existence as living-dead was born in all the villages between the Dâmbovița and the Roterturn Pass. Every unexplained death, every disappearance or kidnapping, was blamed on me, Vlad the Impaler, the Living-Dead Man, the Unburied, while in reality I laid buried alive in a deep cavern, feeding on roots and dirt, snakes and spiders, rats and the bats that hung from the cavern's vaults, buried alive, Navarro, wanted for crimes I did not commit and paying for those I did commit, wanted by the Congregation of the Holy Inquisition, which was convinced that I had indeed not died and that I was perpetrating every crime attributed to me, but where was I? How were they to discover my hiding place among the tombs like stone fingers, marble stakes, at the edge of the Târnava: buried without a name or date by order of the deceased nuncio, erased from the world but suspected of corrupting it? The location of my forced confinement had been jealously guarded in Rome, forgotten or lost, I don't know. The nuncio took the secret with him to his grave. Then the people of Wallachia heard from the ancestral counsel. *A naked girl on horseback is galloping through all the cemeteries of the region, and wherever the horse comes to a stop, that is Vlad's hiding place, and right there we will bury a stake in the Impaler's chest.* One night I finally heard the fateful gallop. I wrapped my arms around myself. On that night alone, I felt frightened, Navarro. The gallop faded. A few hours later the naked girl returned to the place of my prison, opened the iron doors of my horrible papal jail. 'My name is Minea,' she said. 'I dug the spurs into the horse when he was about to stop over your hiding place. That's how I knew that you were imprisoned here. Now come out. I have come to your rescue. You've learned to nourish yourself from the earth. You've learned how to live underground. You've learned how to get by without seeing your own face ever again. When the hunt for you began, I volunteered myself innocently enough. Nobody suspects a ten-year-old girl. I took advantage of my childish appearance, but I have been roaming the night for three centuries. I have come to make a deal with you. Come out of this prison and join us. I offer you eternal life. We are legion. You have found your people. The price you have to pay is very small.' That little girl Minea threw herself on me and buried her teeth in my neck. I had found my people. I am not a creator, Navarro, I am just another creature, do you understand? I was made by that innocent-seeming ten-year-old girl. Like you, I lived in time. Like you, I would have died. The girl ripped me out of time and dragged me into eternity . . ."

He was strangling me.

"Don't you feel any compassion for me? She ripped out my eyes, she sucked them out the way she sucks everything, so that my eyes couldn't express a need for anything other than blood, nor sympathy for anything other than the night . . ."

I tried to bite the hand that gagged me and forced me to listen to this incredible and ancient story, though I feared, like an idiot, that to draw the blood of a vampire was to tempt the devil himself. Vlad tightened his grip over my body.

"Children are all inner strength, Mr. Navarro. A part of our vital force is contained inside each child, and we waste it. We want them to stop being children and to become adults, workers, people 'useful to society.' "

He let out a revolting laugh.

"History! Think about the history I just recounted to you, and tell me if that garbage dump of lies—those screens we erect around the terrified mortality that we call careers, politics, economics, art, even art, Mr. Navarro—can save us from idiocy and from death! Do you know what my plan is? To let your daughter grow up, acquire the shape and beauty of a woman, but never to allow her to stop being a girl, a source of life and purity . . .

"No, Minea will never grow up," he said, sensing my confusion. "She is the eternal girl of the night."

He turned me around so that I faced him, and he showed me his shining gums and his ivory fangs polished into mirrors.

"I am waiting for your daughter to grow up, Navarro. She will stay with me. She will be my . . . girlfriend. One day she will be my wife. She will be brought up to be a vampire."

The evil monster flashed an acerbic smile.

"I don't know if we'll be giving you any grandchildren."

He let me go. He extended his arm and pointed the way.

"Wait for your wife in the living room. And keep in mind one thing. I have been feeding on your wife while the little girl has been growing accustomed to her new home. But I won't want to keep her around much longer. Only just so long as she is useful to me. Frankly, I don't understand what you see in her. *Elle est une femme de ménage!*"

14

I walked like a somnambulist to the white living room with black furniture and numerous drains, and there I sat and waited. When my wife appeared, dressed in black, her hair let down, her gaze fixed, I felt sympathy and antipathy, attraction and repulsion, vast tenderness and an equally great fear.

I stood and offered my hand to draw her closer to me. Asunción rejected the invitation and sat across from me with a vacant look. She didn't touch me.

"Darling," I said, leaning my head and torso forward until my hands clasped my knees, "I've come for you. I've come for our girl. I think all of this is just a nightmare. Let's collect Magda. The car is parked right outside. Asunción, quick, let's get out of here quick."

She looked at me in just the way I had looked at her when she came in, except that she displayed only half of my feelings: antipathy, repulsion, and fear. Which reduced my hand to fear alone.

"Do you love my daughter?" she asked in a new voice that sounded as though she'd swallowed sand, banishing me from our shared parenthood with that cruel, cold possessive: *my* daughter.

"Asunción . . . Magda," I managed to mumble.

"Do you remember Didier?"

"Asunción, he was our son."

"*Is.* He is my son."

"Ours, Asunción. He died. We loved him, we remember him, but he no longer is. He was."

"Magdalena won't die," Asunción declared with an icy calm. "The boy died. The girl will never die. I will never again have to live through that grief."

How, under these circumstances, could I say something to her along the lines of "we're all going to die, someday"—when in my wife's voice and eyes, she had already conjured something like an eternal flame, this belief that she kept repeating . . .

"My daughter will not die. There will be no mourning her. Magdalena will live forever."

Was this her sacrifice? Was this the outer limit of maternal love? Was I supposed to think highly of the mother for making this sacrifice?

"It's not a sacrifice," she said as though she'd been reading my mind. "I am here because of Magda. But I am also here for my own pleasure. I want to make sure you know that."

I recovered my speech then like a bull that has been lanced in the nape of its neck so that it charges all the harder.

"I spoke with that evil old creature," I said.

"Zurinaga? You spoke to Zurinaga?"

This confused me. "Yes, I spoke to Zurinaga too, but I was talking about that other old creature, Vlad . . ."

"I made the deal with Zurinaga," she continued. "Zurinaga was the middleman. He sent Magdalena's picture to Vlad. He offered me the deal in Vladimiro's name . . ."

"Vladimiro," I tried to smile. "He tricked Zurinaga, you know. He offered him eternal life and then sent him straight to hell. The same thing is going to happen to you two."

"He offered me the deal in Vladimiro's name," Asunción continued, ignoring me. "Eternal life for my daughter. Zurinaga knew about my fear. He told Vladimiro all about it."

"In exchange," I interrupted, "you would have sex with Vlad."

For the first time she gave a hint of a smile. Saliva ran down her chin.

"No, even without the girl, I'd choose to be here . . ."

"Asunción," I said, upset. "My adored Asunción, my wife, my love . . ."

"Your love, adored and bored," she said with eyes of black diamond. "Your wife, prisoner of daily tedium."

"Love," I said almost with desperation, certainly with disbelief. "Remember our passionate nights together. How can you say that? You and I, we've loved each other with passion."

"Those are the first moments that are forgotten," she said without moving a muscle in her face. "Your repetitious love is tiresome; your faithfulness, a bore. I've spent years preparing myself for Vladimiro, without knowing it. None of this just happens, as you seem to think, all of a sudden."

Because I had no new words, I repeated the ones I already knew:

"Remember our passion."

"You're so ordinary," she spat out along with the foam that leaked from her lips. "I don't want ordinary."

"Asunción, you're headed for horror, you're going to live in horror, I don't understand you, you're going to be horribly miserable . . ."

She looked at me as if to say "I know," but then she took another tack:

"Yes, I want a man who can hurt me. And you're way too good for that."

She allowed herself a dreadful pause.

"Your faithfulness is a plague."

Having recovered from my astonishment, I played another card. This gambit involved swallowing my pride, its injury overcome thanks to my steadfast love, the true love that celebrates its own limits and loves despite imperfection.

"You're saying all this so that I'll get angry with you, darling, and leave embittered but resigned . . ."

"I'm not a prisoner here," she said, shaking her long lustrous mane, so similar now to the magnificence of Vlad's replenished hair. "No, I have escaped from your prison."

A hissing fury seized her tongue, spreading thick saliva:

"I enjoy being with Vlad. He's a man who instantly knows all a woman's weaknesses . . ."

But that snake's voice ceased as soon as she repeated that she was unable to resist Vlad's attraction. Vlad had broken our life of tedious habit.

"And I'm on fire for him, even though he's only using

me, even though he wants the girl and not me . . ."

Her eyes were shiny with unshed tears.

"Go, Yves, while you still can. You can't stop what's already happening. If you like, you can imagine that, even if I'm hurting you, I will still be fond of you. But get out of here, and as you go on living, ask yourself, which of us has lost more? Did I take more away from you, or you from me? As long as you can't answer that question, you won't know anything about me . . ."

She laughed impudently.

"Go," she said. "Vlad doesn't tolerate shared loyalties."

But I didn't want to give up. I didn't understand the forces I was up against.

"For me, you will always be beautiful, desirable, Asunción . . ."

"No," she lowered her head, "no, not anymore, not for anyone . . ."

"I'm sorry to interrupt this tender domestic scene," Vlad said, appearing suddenly. "The night marches on, and we have duties, my dear Asunción . . ."

At that moment, blood bubbled up from every drain in the living room.

My wife rose and quickly left the room, lifting her skirt over the red puddles.

Vlad looked at me with polite irony.

"May I escort you to the door, Mr. Navarro?"

The automatic responses of my education and my ancestral courtesy cumulatively overcame my weakened resistance. I sat up and walked, led by the Count, to the mansion's door in Bosques de las Lomas.

We crossed the space between the front door and the wrought-iron gate facing the street.

"Don't fight it anymore, Navarro. Ignore the endless advance of death. Be content. Go back to the curse of work, which for you is a blessing. I know and I understand. You live life. I covet life. That's an important distinction. What we have in common is that, in this world, we all use each other. Some of us win, others lose. Accept this."

He put his hand on my shoulder. I shuddered.

"Or join us, Navarro. Yes, why not become a part of my wandering tribe? Look at what I'm offering you, despite your incorruptible pride: stay here with your wife and daughter forever . . . Think about it. If you don't stay with us, you won't see your wife and daughter ever again, you know. Nobody will see them. Nobody but me . . ."

We were in front of the gate, between the street and the house.

"That's not what you want. You'll die without ever seeing them again. Navarro, think it over."

He raised a glassy-fingernailed hand.

"And hurry. Tomorrow we'll be gone. If you go now, you might never see us again. But, then again, do bear in mind that my absence is often deceptive. I always find a weakness, a crack through which I can slip back in, if need be. If such a friend as you, so highly regarded, were to summon me, I would return. I assure you, I'd be there . . ."

My whole being, yes, my schooling, my habits, my entire life, impelled me to choose the work, health, and pleasure that are permitted us human beings. Here was only sickness. Death. Yet, struggling against everything inside me was an intolerable and uncertain tenderness toward this poor creature. He wasn't the origin of evil. He was a victim. He was not born a monster; they turned him into a vampire . . . He was a creature of his daughter, Minea, just another victim, poor Vlad . . .

The cursed Count played his last card.

"Your wife and daughter will live forever. If that alone is of no interest to you, wouldn't you like your son to come back to life too? Would you despise that possibility as well? Don't look at me like that, Navarro. I'm not in the habit of joking about matters of life and death. Look, your car is parked over there. Take a good look and make up your mind quickly. I'm in a hurry to leave."

I looked at him inquiringly.

"You're leaving?"

Vlad answered coldly: "You will forget this place and this day. You were never in this house. Never."

"You're leaving Mexico City?" I asked again, my voice sounding distant and anesthetized.

"No, Navarro. I'm going to lose myself in Mexico City, just as in the past I lost myself in London, in Rome, in Bremerhaven, in New Orleans, wherever my imagination and the fear of mortals like you have led me. Now I will lose myself in perhaps the most populous city on the planet. I will blend in with the nocturnal crowds, already savoring the abundance of fresh blood, ready to make it mine, to resume my thirst, the thirst for the ancient sacrifice that is at the origin of all history . . . But don't forget this: my friends always call me Vlad."

I turned my back on this vampire, on his horror, on his fatalism. *Yes*, I was going to choose life and work, even though my heart had already died forever. And yet, a sacred voice, hidden until that moment, whispered into my ear, from within my soul, that the secret of the world is that it's unfinished, because God himself is unfinished. Perhaps, like the vampire, God is a nocturnal and mysterious being who has not yet manifested or understood Himself, and that is why he needs us. To live so that God doesn't die. To carry on living the unfinished work of a yearning God.

I gave a last sidelong glance at the gully of felled trees that had been turned into stakes. Magda and Minea laughed and swung between the stakes, singing:

> *Sleep, pretty wantons, do not cry,*
> *and I will sing a lullaby:*
> *rock them, rock them, lullaby . . .*

I felt my will to live drained, slipping away like the blood down the drains of the vampire's mansion. I didn't even have the will to accept the deal Vlad had offered. Work, the rewards of life, the pleasures . . . Everything had escaped me. I was defeated by all that remained undone. I felt the pain of the terrible nostalgia for what was not and would never be. What had I lost on this awful day? Not love, which persisted in spite of everything. Not love, but hope. Vlad had left me without hope, with no consolation except to feel that what happened had happened to another, the feeling that everything came from somewhere else, even though it had happened to me: I was the sieve, an intangible mystery had passed through me but had come and gone, from somewhere to somewhere else . . . And yet, might its passage not have changed me nevertheless, and forever?

I went out onto the street.

The wrought-iron gate shut behind me.

I could not resist a final look at Count Vlad's mansion.

Something even stranger than everything I had already seen was happening.

The Bosques de las Lomas house, its airy modern glass façade and its clean geometric lines, were dissolving before my eyes, as if they were melting. As the modern house dissolved, another house appeared little by little in its place, changing the new into the old, glass into stone, the substitution of one form for another.

There was appearing, little by little, behind the veil of the visible house, the shape of an ancient, ruined, uninhabitable castle, already pervaded with that smell I knew from the coffin-lined tunnel: an unstable edifice, creaky like the hull of a very old ship run aground amid rugged mountains, a castle with a ruined watchtower, with eaten-away battlements, with threatening towers flanking it on all sides, with moldy gates, with a dry and slimy moat, and with the highest tower, the tower of homage, bearing the castle's master, Vlad watching me with his dark sunglasses, telling me he would leave this place and that I would never recognize it if I returned, summoning me back into the catacomb, warning me that I would never again be able to live a normal life, no matter how hard I struggled, because despite everything I would know that my life force was already buried in a tomb, that I myself would thenceforth live, wherever I was, in the vampire's tomb, and that however much I affirmed my will to live, I was condemned to death because I would live with the knowledge of what I had undergone so that Vlad's black tribe would not perish.

Then, from a side tower, they flew clumsily away, clumsily because they were like monstrous rats endowed with varicose wings, the blind *Vespertilios*, the bats guided by the power of their filthy, long, hairy ears, emigrating to a new sepulcher.

Were Asunción, my wife, and Magda, my daughter, among the flock of blind rats?

I approached my parked car.

Something was moving inside the vehicle.

Someone.

A blurred figure.

When I could finally make it out, I screamed in a mixture of horror and joy.

I raised my hands to my eyes, I hid my gaze, and I could only mutter:

"No, no, no . . ."

The author of more than a dozen novels and collections of stories and essays, CARLOS FUENTES (1928–2012) was Mexico's most celebrated novelist and critic. He received numerous honors and awards throughout his lifetime, including the Miguel de Cervantes Prize and the Latin Literary Prize.

E. SHASKAN BUMAS wrote the story collection *The Price of Tea in China*, a finalist for PEN America West Fiction Book of the Year. He teaches at New Jersey City University.

ALEJANDRO BRANGER is a writer and filmmaker. He lives in New York City.

PETROS ABATZOGLOU, *What Does Mrs.
Freeman Want?*
MICHAL AJVAZ, *The Golden Age.*
The Other City.
PIERRE ALBERT-BIROT, *Grabinoulor.*
YUZ ALESHKOVSKY, *Kangaroo.*
FELIPE ALFAU, *Chromos.*
Locos.
JOÃO ALMINO, *The Book of Emotions.*
IVAN ÂNGELO, *The Celebration.*
The Tower of Glass.
DAVID ANTIN, *Talking.*
ANTÓNIO LOBO ANTUNES, *Knowledge of Hell.*
The Splendor of Portugal.
ALAIN ARIAS-MISSON, *Theatre of Incest.*
IFTIKHAR ARIF AND WAQAS KHWAJA, EDS.,
Modern Poetry of Pakistan.
JOHN ASHBERY AND JAMES SCHUYLER,
A Nest of Ninnies.
ROBERT ASHLEY, *Perfect Lives.*
GABRIELA AVIGUR-ROTEM, *Heatwave
and Crazy Birds.*
HEIMRAD BÄCKER, *transcript.*
DJUNA BARNES, *Ladies Almanack.*
Ryder.
JOHN BARTH, *LETTERS.*
Sabbatical.
DONALD BARTHELME, *The King.*
Paradise.
SVETISLAV BASARA, *Chinese Letter.*
MIQUEL BAUÇÀ, *The Siege in the Room.*
RENÉ BELLETTO, *Dying.*
MAREK BIEŃCZYK, *Transparency.*
MARK BINELLI, *Sacco and Vanzetti
Must Die!*
ANDREI BITOV, *Pushkin House.*
ANDREJ BLATNIK, *You Do Understand.*
LOUIS PAUL BOON, *Chapel Road.*
My Little War.
Summer in Termuren.
ROGER BOYLAN, *Killoyle.*
IGNÁCIO DE LOYOLA BRANDÃO,
Anonymous Celebrity.
The Good-Bye Angel.
Teeth under the Sun.
Zero.
BONNIE BREMSER, *Troia: Mexican Memoirs.*
CHRISTINE BROOKE-ROSE, *Amalgamemnon.*
BRIGID BROPHY, *In Transit.*
MEREDITH BROSNAN, *Mr. Dynamite.*
GERALD L. BRUNS, *Modern Poetry and
the Idea of Language.*
EVGENY BUNIMOVICH AND J. KATES, EDS.,
*Contemporary Russian Poetry:
An Anthology.*
GABRIELLE BURTON, *Heartbreak Hotel.*
MICHEL BUTOR, *Degrees.*
Mobile.
Portrait of the Artist as a Young Ape.
G. CABRERA INFANTE, *Infante's Inferno.*
Three Trapped Tigers.
JULIETA CAMPOS,
The Fear of Losing Eurydice.
ANNE CARSON, *Eros the Bittersweet.*
ORLY CASTEL-BLOOM, *Dolly City.*
CAMILO JOSÉ CELA, *Christ versus Arizona.*
The Family of Pascual Duarte.
The Hive.
LOUIS-FERDINAND CÉLINE, *Castle to Castle.*
Conversations with Professor Y.
London Bridge.

Normance.
North.
Rigadoon.
MARIE CHAIX, *The Laurels of Lake Constance.*
HUGO CHARTERIS, *The Tide Is Right.*
JEROME CHARYN, *The Tar Baby.*
ERIC CHEVILLARD, *Demolishing Nisard.*
LUIS CHITARRONI, *The No Variations.*
MARC CHOLODENKO, *Mordechai Schamz.*
JOSHUA COHEN, *Witz.*
EMILY HOLMES COLEMAN, *The Shutter
of Snow.*
ROBERT COOVER, *A Night at the Movies.*
STANLEY CRAWFORD, *Log of the S.S. The
Mrs Unguentine.*
Some Instructions to My Wife.
ROBERT CREELEY, *Collected Prose.*
RENÉ CREVEL, *Putting My Foot in It.*
RALPH CUSACK, *Cadenza.*
SUSAN DAITCH, *L.C.*
Storytown.
NICHOLAS DELBANCO, *The Count of Concord.*
Sherbrookes.
NIGEL DENNIS, *Cards of Identity.*
PETER DIMOCK, *A Short Rhetoric for
Leaving the Family.*
ARIEL DORFMAN, *Konfidenz.*
COLEMAN DOWELL,
The Houses of Children.
Island People.
Too Much Flesh and Jabez.
ARKADII DRAGOMOSHCHENKO, *Dust.*
RIKKI DUCORNET, *The Complete
Butcher's Tales.*
The Fountains of Neptune.
The Jade Cabinet.
The One Marvelous Thing.
Phosphor in Dreamland.
The Stain.
The Word "Desire."
WILLIAM EASTLAKE, *The Bamboo Bed.*
Castle Keep.
Lyric of the Circle Heart.
JEAN ECHENOZ, *Chopin's Move.*
STANLEY ELKIN, *A Bad Man.*
Boswell: A Modern Comedy.
*Criers and Kibitzers, Kibitzers
and Criers.*
The Dick Gibson Show.
The Franchiser.
George Mills.
The Living End.
The MacGuffin.
The Magic Kingdom.
Mrs. Ted Bliss.
The Rabbi of Lud.
Van Gogh's Room at Arles.
FRANÇOIS EMMANUEL, *Invitation to a
Voyage.*
ANNIE ERNAUX, *Cleaned Out.*
SALVADOR ESPRIU, *Ariadne in the
Grotesque Labyrinth.*
LAUREN FAIRBANKS, *Muzzle Thyself.*
Sister Carrie.
LESLIE A. FIEDLER, *Love and Death in
the American Novel.*
JUAN FILLOY, *Faction.*
Op Oloop.
ANDY FITCH, *Pop Poetics.*
GUSTAVE FLAUBERT, *Bouvard and Pécuchet.*
KASS FLEISHER, *Talking out of School.*

SELECTED DALKEY ARCHIVE TITLES

FOR A FULL LIST OF PUBLICATIONS, VISIT:
www.dalkeyarchive.com

FOR A FULL LIST OF PUBLICATIONS, VISIT:
www.dalkeyarchive.com